REAPER

DEATH ROW SHOOTERS MC

CRIMSON SYN

DEAR READERS

Hello my lovely readers!

Thank you for joining me and for following me into the gritty world of the Death Row Shooters MC. I really wanted this storyline to interconnect with the Hellbound Lovers so be prepared to see some more of your favorite characters in this series.

This book starts off two weeks after the occurrences of the war between the Colombian Cartel and the Hellbound Lovers MC where we first met Ryan Simon. If you followed that storyline then you know that he helped Wolf Stone when his family was in danger.

But now Ryan is back and he wants something in return. Something he gave to Wolf a long time ago, and he wants it at all costs. Our Reaper is a broken man, a solitary soul, with only one purpose in life-to get back his Firefly.

Thrown into a life of criminal activity. He has seen and been a part of death for such a long time, spilling blood is only a natural repercussion of survival. But this isn't the life he wanted for himself, especially not after meeting Cecilia.

She is everything he ever wanted. His light, his innocence, all wrapped up in a beautiful woman. A woman he has to give up in order to save her life.

Sinful Reading,

Crimson Syn

GLOSSARY OF TERMS

La Muerte:Death

La Plaga: The Plague

La Mancha: The Stain

La Sombra: The Shadow

Pendejo:Idiot

Coño: Fuck

Eres un traidor de mierda!: You're a traitorous shit!

Muevete:Move

Linda: Pretty girl

Puta Mentirosa: Lying bitch

Niña: Little girl

cabrón: fucker

No soy tan pendejo: I'm not that much of an idiot.

Mi Reina: My queen

Hijo de Puta!: Son of a Bitch

Muerete!: Die

PROLOGUE

RYAN

Present Day...

My name is Ryan Simon, known among the brotherhood as The Reaper. Why the nickname, you ask? Because I have this bad tendency of sending men to their graves. Specifically, vile evil men who hurt the ones I love. My first kill alone made me the cold calculating bastard I am today. I'm a man with powerful connections who fears no one and nothing. I am the President of the Death Row Shooters MC.

I'm not going to spin you into a web of fairy tales and fancy dreams. My life is shit and continues to be shit. From the moment I stepped foot into that goddamn place and became a Prospect, my life turned into a nightmare. Thievery, rape, death, and bloodshed. I have to admit I learned everything I know from the evil that took me in. I found out what darkness felt like. How it consumes you. And instead of fighting it, I used it. But in the midst of all the shit that was thrown at me, I also learned what brotherhood meant. What it still means to me to this day.

I've tried to change my ways, but it's hard when this is all I've ever known. I've delved in drug trafficking, prostitution, and even money laundering. After I lost the last of my family in that goddamn shooting I knew I couldn't lose anymore loved ones. There was only one person that mattered to me more than life itself. The only person in this world who truly knew who I was. This one special person I had sworn to protect. I didn't even know where she was kept hidden, but I was about to find out.

As I glared at the man sitting across from me, I knew this wasn't going to be easy. "You know what I'm going to ask, and I know I told you never to tell me, but fuck, I need to know."

Wolf Stone, the President of the Hellbound Lovers MC, stared back at me, a sullen expression on his face. He paused for a long time, long enough for me to see the wheels spinning in his head. He was sharp, unforgiving, and loyal as fuck. And he knew that I had done everything in my power to keep his ass safe in the last year and it was time to pay it back.

"There's always a price to pay, Wolf. It's just your turn to pay it."

Wolf shook his head in disgust. "You're a motherfucker."

I smirked. "I won't deny that."

"She's not ready to be found, Ryan."

"That's not your decision to make."

Wolf curled his lip and grimaced. "You goddamn know it is. She was handed over to the Hellbound Lovers which means she is our responsibility."

"Goddammit, Wolf! She's mine, I want her back!"

In my built-up anger, I hurled the highball glass I was holding. It flew across the room and shattered against the wall behind Wolf's head, yet the fucker didn't even flinch. We stared at each other in a long, intensely charged moment. The tension rose in the room while I glared at him, seething in anger.

"It's been six years, Wolf."

"I know how long it's been. She's not ready."

"I'm gonna play nice and ask this as a favor here. I need to see her."

Wolf sighed and tilted his head assessing me and my apparently desperate condition. "Let's do this. I'll ask her if she wants to see you. If she agrees, I'll set up a time and place for you to meet. But if she says no..."

"She won't say no."

"But if she does..."

I charged at Wolf and he stood up, his massive size ready for a fight. I pulled up toe to toe with him, my hands fisting at my sides. I was a big guy, by every means, but Wolf was built like a Marine. I held my own in a fight, but he could kill me with a snap of his wrist and the fucker knew it. He had a level head and I was well aware I was testing his limits.

"If she says no I'll go looking for her my goddamn self! And I will find her," I was fuming; hating that Wolf was keeping what I wanted from me.

He shook his head slowly. "If she says no, this ends here. Understood?"

I stared back at Wolf and I felt my blood run cold. I liked him, he was a great friend, but he was an even more formidable adversary. He wasn't one to mess with, but who ever said I gave a fuck.

"I don't want to get into it with you, Wolf. I just want

back what belongs to me. You were supposed to hide her from her father and that fucker La Plaga. They are now dead, I made sure of it. There's no reason for her to keep living in fear."

"She's not. She's aware of what' happened. She's perfectly content with her life, Ryan. She's at peace. Why would you want to disrupt that?"

"Because I'm her fucking peace!" I slammed my fist against my chest in anger.

"Calm. The fuck. Down."

For a brief moment, just a small one, I hated Wolf Stone. I hated that he had what was mine. But what I hated even more was that he was being fucking loyal...to me! The man who handed her over. The man, who above all else, only sought out her protection.

I tried staring him down, but it was no use. Wolf wasn't the type to be easily threatened. He only sat back down, leaned back in the chair, folded his arms across his massive chest and waited. Waited for me to calm down, to realize that what I was doing was completely out of character, to acknowledge that she was better off alone.

But that wasn't going to happen. Because I was a greedy bastard. I'd waited six long fucking years to be able to finally claim what was mine. Six long, lonely years.

I slumped down in the seat across from his and cradled my head in my hands. "Just give her back, Wolf."

I heard his sigh of resignation. "I'll ask her, but I won't force her to see you."

I raised my head, my eyes meeting his stoic gaze. "If she doesn't come willingly I will go after her. You know I'd never hurt her, but she needs to know that I'm here, that I'm waiting. That I've been waiting."

I stood up, but before he could say another word, I

stormed out of his office. Stepping out into the chilled morning air, I shuddered. The door slammed shut behind me, echoing in the silence. I looked back at Ravenous, looming over me in the dark. The only light came from a single streetlamp that casted its dim yellow light in front of the entrance and shed the rest of the street in a dark ominous shadow. Where anyone else would feel threatened by the emptiness, I felt at home.

It was nearing four in the morning and everyone had gone home for the night. I straightened my suit jacket, adjusted my black silk tie and made my way to my BMR R nine T Pure. She was my baby and it had taken me years to finally get a bike that I wanted, completely customized to my taste and believe me, I had an expensive palette.

What I owned, I shed my own blood and sweat for. I had put my life on the line for everything I had, as well as for who I had by my side. I didn't need anything. Never did. I could have anything I wanted, whenever I wanted it. Anything...but her. I wasn't going to take no for an answer. Revving up the bike I sat there for a moment, staring off into nothing, remembering the last time I'd seen her. She'd been so young, so innocent, yet exposed to so much fucked up shit. That night was the start of a long battle, a night where I gave up my soul to Wolf Stone, a night where I put my life on the line for the woman I loved. I waited enough time for her and now I want her back, and no Hellbound Lover was going to get in my way.

1

RYAN

Nine Years Ago…

I was fourteen years old when I was taken in as a Prospect for the Death Row Shooters. It wasn't the life I had initially wanted but it was the one that was handed to me. In one night, my cousin Simon had become my legal guardian, and the only family I had left in this fucking world. Nate Schear was the President back then, and the Death Row Shooters were held in high regard and well respected. But in the last four years, shit had changed. Mario *La Muerte* Cepeda was now the elected President and he ran this club like he did his life, down the fucking shitter. Simon should have gotten the title as VP, but there was only one reason this fucker got chosen, and it was because he brought in the pussy. That's how he won half the brothers over, the other half left after Nate died. A fucking shame.

We'd been told he was drunk driving down the highway and he swerved right into a truck. Fucked up part about that shit was that we all knew it was a lie, but no one did anything about it. Nate rarely drank, and he would be the first one to tell us to be careful on that road. He'd been a good man, taken me in when I didn't have anywhere else to go, and he offered me refuge. Him being gone only made the tension in the club worse and by the time the funeral was over, half the brothers had started a new chapter somewhere far from Sacramento.

Being a Prospect wasn't all rainbows and butterflies, I'd seen the worst of the worst growing up under La Muerte's tyrannous reign. Drug trafficking, gun trafficking, money laundering, death, blood, gore, torture, you name it. Fuck, I shot my first victim during a drug deal that went wrong. It was either shoot the dealer or risk him snitching us out. I didn't even think twice about it. I was fifteen years old.

My first fuck was with a thirty-year-old prostitute named Savannah. She wasn't the prettiest of the hookers that hung out at the bar, but she was the nicest. At sixteen I had no idea what the hell I was doing, and she taught me it didn't really matter as long as I didn't cum too early. That first time was in the back alley behind the dumpsters, the smell of rotten food and stale beer hit my nostrils as she slobbered around my teenage dick. I remember thinking *I'd show them,* as I stuck my cock in a woman who kept moaning daddy with a sixteen-year-old attempting to fuck her from behind. At least I didn't cum early. Afterwards, La Muerte congratulated me for becoming a man and patted me on the back welcoming me into the brotherhood.

I stayed because of Simon, I owed him that. Fuck, I owed him my life. See, Simon was the only one who had been there for me when my mother left this earth. I remember that night clearly, as if it were yesterday. I had gotten home late from school that day. When I walked in I saw my mother's boyfriend, Mitch, in the kitchen. I'd hated Mitch from the start, there was something wrong with him, but there was no reasoning with my mother, so I left it alone. He grunted at me when I walked in, but I never acknowledged the asshole. I watch him grimace as my ma' set a plate of food down in front of him. She'd looked up and smiled at me. I can still smell that scent of fresh baked cookies and dishwashing soap that always swirled around her. She kissed me hello as he began to complain about the meatloaf being too cold.

Sighing, she told me to run upstairs and wash my hands. I was only gone a few minutes, but I wish I'd never left her side. I blame myself every fucking day for leaving her alone with him. Maybe if I would have been present, things would have been different.

Some nights I can still hear her curdling scream. I nearly tumbled down the stairs trying to get to her, but it had been too late. She was lying in the hallway, blood pouring from her head out onto the hardwood floor. Mitch standing over her, seething in anger. His eyes met mine as I flew to her side.

"She made me do it! You should have seen her! She fucking attacked me!"

I ignored him and tried to shake her awake. "Momma? Momma wake up. Wake up, momma!"

I looked up just as Mitch ran out the front door leaving it wide open, my cousin Simon in the doorway staring down at me. His eyes said it all, a murderous glare in them as he lifted me away from her. He checked her pulse and hung his head.

"Go pack a bag, Ry, we gotta go."

"But what about Ma! We have to call the cops and ambulance!"

"Just do as I say!" He yelled, shoving me towards the stairs. I looked down at my mother and watched as Simon brushed his hand along her face, closing her eyes. That's when I knew. Momma was gone.

As Simon tied my bag to the back of his bike, he handed me a helmet. "Where are we going?"

"Someplace safe, now stop asking questions and get on."

He tapped the helmet and I gripped his leather jacket as he took me away from my home, away from everything I knew. I never saw Mitch again, nor did we speak of my mother. I heard from Poe and Ash that Simon had taken care of that son of a bitch and I didn't have to worry about a thing. I was pretty sure he was buried six feet under in the middle of the woods somewhere. I hoped he'd cut him up in little pieces and left him for the wolves. I'm morbid that way.

Poe Chambers was also a Prospect, he'd been brought in by Simon. An underground boxer, he was left for dead on the side of the road when he decided he wasn't going to listen to his fucking boss and he won a fight he was supposed to throw. The Mexican cartel lost a lot of money that night, and he paid for it costly, they shattered his right hand, but he had a mean left hook, so the joke was on them. Simon brought him in and Poe was forever grateful. He was older than me by a few years, quiet, but resourceful, and he was loyal as fuck. He'd been called the Poet in the boxing ring after a newspaper article had claimed that it was fucking poetic watching him bring down a man with his fists. The title stuck.

Ashley Warden, better known round here as Ash, was Nate's nephew and the Death Row Shooters Enforcer. God forbid you called him by his God given name, he'd probably shoot you on the spot. The only one allowed to call him that was his mother, and she'd been dead ten years. He'd been a Fire Marshall a few years back, had gotten injured during a bad fire, the flames scarred him along the right side of his torso, and in the end, he had been the only survivor that night. He later got kicked out for getting drunk at a bar and starting a major fight. Eight men injured, one dead. It wasn't his fault, but he'd done five years for reckless behavior. When he got out he called Nate, and he was patched in immediately, no questions asked. Ash was a ruthless bastard, but a good man to have at your back.

Then there was Cecilia Cepedo, the light in all this fucking darkness. If there was anyone I couldn't dare leave, it was her, my Angel, my Firefly. When La Muerte brought Cecilia to live with the Death Row Shooters we all thought he'd gone crazy, but he was dead serious. Her grandmother had recently died, her mother was a druggie who got lost on the streets, and she had nowhere to go. Mario hated her, the boys and I took her in as a little sister. But she meant more to me than that, even at my eighteen years I knew this. I felt protective of the girl. I always wanted her around and when she wasn't, I sought her out. She was everything I wasn't at fifteen. Sweet, pure, full of life. I didn't want Mario to blemish her, but I knew it was only a matter of time. The disgusting piece of shit kept ogling her whenever he got the chance. At first, I thought I was seeing things, but then I caught him rubbing his cock while watching her doing her homework one afternoon. The fucker repulsed me, but when I told Simon he told me to mind my own damn business unless I wanted to eat bullet shells for dinner.

So, I kept my mouth shut, but I stayed vigilant of her, and I knew that no matter what, my brothers had my back. Simon especially. I could tell after I spoke with him, that there was a change in him. He became more rebellious, more defiant, and half the time he was biting his tongue trying to keep out of La Muerte's way. But he'd taken note of what I'd witnessed, and he kept his eye on Cecilia, just as Poe and Ash did. She didn't deserve this life, she'd been ripped out of her own home and dragged here, the least we could do was keep her safe.

It wasn't long until Simon was brought down from his charge as VP and made Tail Gunner. He never said a word though, always kept his mouth shut. Never said anything when we were told lies about Nate's death, never spoke up about being President, and he never said a word about them stripping him of his title. He told me once that he knew what he was doing. These fuckers went after your family first, and he wasn't about to risk that.

That's what she was to me, my Cecilia. She was family, and I'd do anything to protect her. Unfortunately, I wasn't always around. It wasn't until this particular afternoon that I knew that I'd do anything in my power to strip Mario *La Muerte* Cepeda of everything he had.

"Hey Ry!"

"Hey, Firefly, how was school?"

I was wiping down the glasses at the bar and it had been pretty quiet in the clubhouse for a few hours now. I liked this time of day. I got my daily dose of Cecilia's day, followed by stories of her classes and friends, and every once in a while, she'd sit quietly at the corner of the bar and finish her homework. I liked her presence near me, it brought me peace and a sense of normalcy.

"It was alright. Same old shit."

"What did I tell you about cursing?"

"What? You curse all the time."

"Yeah, but I'm allowed."

"I'm fifteen Ryan, I'm not a child." She looked around and frowned. "Where is everyone?"

"They went out on a job, they should be back soon."

She hesitated for a moment. "Did my dad go with them?"

"No. He's in the back somewhere. Why?"

"No reason." The nervous tilt to her tone put me on edge.

Had he done something to her? Had he touched her?

I set the rag down and leaned in towards her pretty face, and my God was she pretty. Her light blue eyes, a complete contrast to my darker ones, shined back at me, perfect pink lips, a heart shaped face. She really did look like an angel with her golden hair that flowed down to her waistline. She had it in a pretty braid today which I grabbed to pull her in closer. I liked the way her eyes went wide and innocent.

"You know you could tell me anything, right?" I whispered.

Her eyes fell, and a blush highlighted her cheeks. Damn, was she cute.

"I'm okay."

"You sure? Cause if you weren't..." my breath caught for a second with thoughts that crossed my mind of of the vile things they could do to her. "I'd do anything for you, Firefly."

Her eyes met mine and I could tell she was holding something back. It was right there in her eyes, but she never had a chance. Her father's booming voice startled us and I watched her stiffen in her seat, barely moving.

"There's my little girl! Come here Cecilia, I want to show you something." He glared at me while she reluctantly approached him, her shoulders slumped forward. He placed his arm around her, and she visibly recoiled from his touch. I knew she hated him, after all the things he's done to her. He wasn't a father. He was a monster.

"Finish up and go, Turner. I don't need you around these parts. I want to spend some time with my little girl." He wrapped her braid around his fist and I clenched the rag.

Don't touch her you fucking piece of shit.

I wanted to rip her away from his hands, hide her. But I kept my mouth shut like Simon had taught me to do.

Bide your time, Ry. Everyone falls one way or another.

I watched as he lead her up the stairs towards his bedroom. I knew what his intentions were, so as soon as he shut the door, I ran up behind them. Pressing my back against the wall by the door, I strained to hear something, anything.

Scream, Cecilia. Don't stay quiet. Yell out for me.

I waited and sure enough there were shouts and then a scuffle, something was toppled over and that's when I heard her cry, followed by the crude sound of flesh slapping flesh. I didn't even think about it, I was always compulsive, and as I swung the door open I froze at the sight before me. The glass I'd been holding cracked and shattered in my hand, cutting it open, but I didn't even feel the pain, let alone the blood that was dripping down my fingers.

"Get the fuck out!"

Mario Cepeda had his daughter over his lap, her tear-stricken face staring back at me, a plea in her eyes. Her underwear was ripped, and his hand was on her round bottom, gripping it tightly. She flinched and whimpered, and he tugged on her braid. "Sit the fuck still! You do as I say and if you disobey me again you'll pay with your life."

He knocked her down to the floor and she fell on her knees with a loud thump. Her skirt was torn and it barely covered her. She sat on her knees and big drops of tears streamed down her cheeks, her eyes never meeting mine. Mario Cepeda chuckled in the distance and I my eyes landed on him as he pulled his zipper up.

"I guess your little boyfriend here doesn't understand the meaning of get out."

I heard the cock of the gun, and I waited. Maybe a bullet would help me unsee the atrocities I had just witnessed. I turned to the disgusting pig and was about to show him just how he could rot in hell when my cousin placed a hand on my shoulder.

"You're bleeding. What the hell?"

He turned me around, his eyes meeting mine filled with concern and an unspoken language that only he and I understood. *Keep your mouth shut*, he was screaming at me as he tended to my wound.

I heard Mario sigh as he placed the gun on the table with a heavy thump. Simon looked up, his eyes narrowing when they landed on Cecilia. "What the hell's going on in here?"

"None of your goddamn business!"

Simon stood there, a stoic glare in his eye. Anyone else would fear that look, anyone but Mario. He thought he was above everyone, even my cousin. If he only knew that Simon was simmering inside, and that if he wasn't careful, one wrong move would lead him right to his grave.

"I need to talk to you about the deal."

"Fuck!" Mario stroked his long unkempt beard and looked down at Cecilia. "Get out!"

He was now aggravated at her and grimaced as she tried to get up. Simon strolled over to her and lifted her gently. I heard her whimper and watched with a broken heart as she faltered. He guided her back to me and leaned her against me while he placed pressure on my hand with the rag and raised it up to my chest.

"I'll clean this shit up, go." He grabbed me by the shoulders and looked at me. "Take her." I turned and slowly made my way out of the room. As soon as the door slammed behind us, she slumped against me. I lifted her and carried her to the top of the steps. Sitting on the corner I cradled her.

"I'm so sorry, Firefly. I'm so fucking sorry."

Her sobs echoed in the silence and I felt my heart break for her not knowing that it wouldn't be the last time it would break for my Cecilia.

2

CECILIA

Six Years ago...

I HAD A THING FOR RYAN TURNER. THE CLUB OFFICER did things to my insides, made me want things, naughty things. He was so damn gorgeous with his short dark blonde hair, and those dark blue eyes of his. God, I loved his eyes. I was crushing, and I was crushing hard. It was his birthday today, he was turning twenty-one. I wanted to do something special for him, and with the money I'd saved in the last few months from bar backing I was hoping he liked his gift. Mario, my father, let me keep the tips and every penny I earned I kept hidden. You never knew with him. Any little thing would make him snap, and he would take my money away in a heartbeat. He was never kind, never affectionate, and the way he looked at me always gave me chills. I tried to stay away as much as possible and now that I was eighteen, I couldn't wait to have enough money saved to leave.

After the first few months, Mario had refused to keep paying for school, telling me it was a waste of money because I was worthless like my mother. Ash and Ryan were the ones who'd helped me and had offered to place me in a public school. It wasn't the private school I was accustomed to, but at least I was going to be able to graduate this year. Ryan had been so proud of me, and to celebrate he'd taken me out for dinner and a movie, just us. He'd held my hand the entire time and I swore I'd never forget that night. But tonight, was his night, and I wanted it to be special. I was baking him a cake and I'd asked Ash and Poe for help with ordering dinner. Simon had paid for it all. We were having a small celebration in a little while but before then I needed to give him his gift.

I paced the back alleyway where I'd texted him to meet me. It was slightly cool out, and the wind had picked up sending goosebumps. up along my bare legs. I hated the outfits my father made me wear. The shortest miniskirts and the tightest tank tops. I wasn't allowed to change it either. The last and only time I'd gone against him, he'd dumped beer all over me and made fun of me in front of the whole bar. I was ridiculed and embarrassed as he continued to yell how it was a wet titty contest. He was so fucking crude. Shocked, I just stood there, while another one of the members, Morgue, that's what they called him, had dumped more beer on me. I held back tears, gasping as it drenched me head to toe.

When he reached out to touch my breasts, Simon had gripped him by the wrist and told him that if he dared to come near me again, he'd cut off his balls. He put his arm around me and walked me away as everyone heckled and laughed at me. When Ryan found out, he'd been livid, and kicked the living shit out of Morgue that same night. It wasn't a fair fight, but he got the point across when he sent him to the hospital.

Ryan had always been there for me, and tonight, I wanted to show him just how much I loved having him in my life. How much I loved him. I wasn't sure how he was going to take it, he was always so quiet, so serious, and he hated surprises. But this feeling between us deserved more, it deserved to be fought for.

"Hey!"

I twirled around to find him running down the alley towards me. He wasn't wearing his jacket and his black t-shirt molded to his cut broad chest. Tattoos ran up the length of one arm and I knew they ran across his shoulder blades. He was working on his chest piece and I couldn't wait to see it. I just wanted to run my fingers across his body, tracing each and every single piece of art.

I smiled at him as he got closer feeling that thrill that gave me butterflies when he was near. He ran his hand across his locks and gave me a sexy lopsided smile back. "You wanted to see me, Firefly?"

I swallowed hard at the nickname. If he only knew just how much I loved hearing it. "Umm...I got you something. I just didn't want to give it to you inside."

"Oh. You didn't have to do that, babe."

I met his eyes and frowned. "Yes I do."

He smirked. "Okay. Whatever my sweet girl says."

Going over to my bag, I took out the small black box. I held it tightly in my hands for a few seconds before whirling around. His nearness made me gasp as the back of my fingers grazed his taut stomach. I blushed as he stared down at me, those eyes of his always so damn intense.

"Whatcha got there, Cecilia?"

"Y-your gift." I raised it up so he could see it. He arched a brow as he took it from my hands. His eyes never left mine while he slid open the black satin ribbon. Lifting the lid he finally glanced down at the item. I was nervous, waiting to see what he'd say.

Inside of the box was a black leather bracelet with a silver clasp. On the front of the clasp was the Death Row Shooters logo, and along the inside of the leather band was a silver plate that I had engraved.

To my Savior, Your Firefly, Forever.

I waited, but when he didn't say a word, I started to get anxious. He simply stared down at the item in his hand, biting down on his lip in silence. I wrung my fingers and finally, not able to take the suspense any longer, I broke the silence.

"Do you like it?"

He looked at me then and the look in his eyes startled me. His glare seared me, and I felt it go straight to my core. There were no words for what he did next, just a wave of fervor that emanated from him and assaulted my senses. Lifting me into his arms he slammed us against the side of the building. He paused for a second and then his lips were finally touching mine, teasing them open until I had the taste of his tongue on my own. A delicious warmth spread through me as he tugged me closer, my breasts tingling against his chest, my lips trembling. His kiss was firm yet sweet, tasting and teasing me. I gasped as he tangled his tongue with mine. His hand cupping the back of my head, holding it in place as he molded my inexperienced lips to his. There was a wordless need in the sighs we breathed.

I fisted his shirt as he pressed his hips to mine, a seductive union that made my toes curl. He was gentle yet firm, letting me know that this was a long time coming. With a low groan he broke the kiss, still lingering as he swept his lips lightly against my mouth.

"You taste like vanilla," he murmured.

I gasped as his hand on my waist tightened, pressing me flush to his body. I wrapped my arms around his neck, his forehead pressed to mine.

"Thank you," his response was earnest and genuine.

I looked down and he had the bracelet in his hand. I took it from him, and with shaky fingers, I wrapped it around his wrist securing the clasp. He stared down at it and a small smile appeared on his lips. He looked like a child receiving a new toy. Looking up at me he gently leaned in and kissed my forehead.

"Best gift ever."

I laughed and before I could help myself, the words spilled out. "Which one? Me or the bracelet." My eyes went wide, and I covered my mouth in shock.

"The bracelet, of course." He laughed as I playfully swatted at his ribs. He grunted and took a step away from me, instantly making me regret playing around with him. I wanted him close.

He grabbed my hand and squeezed it, tugging me towards him. His hands came around me and his lips grazed mine softly, featherlike.

"I've been wanting to kiss you for years, Firefly." He traced my lips with the pad of his thumb, and I shivered.

"You had to have known."

I smiled and blushed. "I wasn't sure. I mean-I know I wanted to. I just didn't think you saw me in that way."

He frowned and I swept my fingers along his furrowed brow, running my fingertips along the contours of his cheeks and chiseled jawline, tracing the outline of his handsome face.

"I want to do a lot more than kiss you, baby. I want to run my tongue along every inch of you and hear you moan my name."

I gasped as he dragged his tongue along my upper lip. "I want to taste you in ways no man will ever get a chance to. Cause you're mine, Firefly."

I raised an eyebrow, placing my hands on my hips. "Oh, is that so?"

He shrugged. His eyes playful. "You really don't have a say in this. I claimed your pretty little ass a long time ago."

He lifted his wrist and grinned, his smile making my heart melt. "Besides, you engraved it, right here." He tapped the leather and I blushed.

"Dammit." I sighed. "And here I thought I was just claiming *my* portion of you."

He growled and pushed me up against the wall, caging me in. His lips hovering over mine while I gripped his belt and tugged him closer.

"Careful, little girl. You're asking for a lot more than I'm willing to resist right now."

I leaned into him and smiled against his lips. "I want it all."

Just as his lips came down on mine the side door slammed open against the brick wall. I screamed and jumped away while my father stood seething in the doorway.

"What the fuck are you doing to my daughter?"

Ryan didn't budge as he leaned on the wall beside me. I turned towards his arm, hiding myself against it. "We were just talking."

I looked at Ryan and I could tell he was pissed. His jaw kept ticking as he spoke to the man who claimed to be my father. "Cecilia, get the fuck inside and get to work!"

"She ain't working tonight," Ryan responded, and I covered my mouth as I watched them interact. It was like watching oil and water mix and I was just waiting to see what would happen when they were both at that boiling point.

"Get inside!" Mario shouted and usually I'd run in, but this time I aimed to be rebellious.

"I said she's staying right here. With me," he whispered to me.

"You will be severely punished for this," he seethed and I knew he was staring right at me. His punishments entailed his leather belt lately, and he'd smack it against my ass whenever he deemed it necessary. If I was lucky I'd be wearing jeans, but he seemed to grab me when I was working so he could raise my skirt and fondle me. I knew it was wrong. I almost threw up that first time. After that it just got worse and worse. He told me he'd kill Ryan if I ever said a word, and I would rather take it to my grave than lose the man I loved.

Ryan gave him a murderous side glance. "We'll see about that."

The tension in the air rose and Ryan pushed off the wall and faced my father while I hid like a coward behind his broad back.

"You challenging me, penned?"

Ryan tensed and I placed my hand on the middle of his back. "No," I whispered, and he instantly relaxed against me.

"I'm leaving." He grabbed my hand and without another word he started walking towards Simon's bike that was parked up on the side. I didn't even look back. In that moment there was not one soul on this earth who could separate me from him. I knew the consequences were going to be harsh, but I was willing to take them as long as I could be with him. I could handle anything as long as he stayed by my side.

3

RYAN

Six Years Ago…

We took the winding roads up to Lake Tahoe, a good two-hour ride. The sun was just setting as I eased the bike down a trail and parked it under the red oaks. Taking her hand in mine, we walked down to the water's edge enjoying the silence. Skunk Harbor was quiet tonight, and we were hidden away in our own attempt at freedom. I never thought I'd never have this moment with her, and for some reason I felt as if though I needed to make it last for both our sakes. I leaned back on a log that stood by the waterfront and pulled her against me, my cock nestled against her belly, her head on my chest.

Was this it?

Was this going to be the night?

I wasn't prepared for this. I thought I was, but I won't lie, I was freaking out. This was Cecilia, my precious girl, the possibility of having her was just unbelievable to me. The thought fluttered into my mind and realization hit.

Why would she ever want with someone like me?

I stopped stroking her back and stared down at my hands. Hands that were rough and overworked, hands that had already taken the lives of others. I wasn't worthy of her and I knew it.

"Ryan?" She looked at me then, those pretty blues shining in the failing sunlight. I couldn't do this to her. Not me.

"Let's go," I grabbed her hand and started walking towards the bike.

"Where are we going?"

"I'm taking you home."

"You brought me here for that?" She jerked her hand away and stopped.

I slowly turned to her. "What are you talking about? What else did you want to happen here? Let's go."

"Ryan," she whispered my name and I clenched my fists tightly. I knew what she wanted. My name falling from her lips said it all.

"I can't touch you, Firefly. If I do there's no turning back."

I felt her hand on my shoulder just before she stepped up to me, searching my face while I avoided her eyes. Cupping my cheeks, she forced me to look at her. "I want this with you. Now, give me what I want," she pouted, and I nearly laughed.

"You're a brat," I growled and dragged her up against the nearest tree.

"I want to be yours, Ryan."

"You don't know what you're asking me to do here, baby."

She smiled up at me then, those big innocent eyes held their secrets, and the next words that slipped off her tongue made my cock pulse. "I want to feel your hands on me, Ryan. Touch me. Please," she whimpered that last word and by God I couldn't help myself. That was it for me. Her admission was what brought me to my knees.

The kiss roused every inch of my body, a breath of lust travelled through us as I tasted her sweet vanilla scent on my tongue. Her moans were laced with sweet little exhales of more. I whirled us around, my mouth on her neck as I practically carried her towards the tree line. Taking my leather off I lay her down on the sandy ground.

I hovered over her, her golden hair spread out around her, her lips swollen and pink from my kisses. She squirmed slightly under my scrutiny and I liked that I did that to her, that I made her slightly uncomfortable. When she bit her lip, I imagined her mouth wrapped around my cock and I felt it leak in my jeans. Her tits shook gently as she moved around beneath me, and I groped one, slowly fondling the nipple, fascinated at how hard it got just from my touch. At the sight of the slight hardened peak, I leaned in and flicked it with my tongue, teasing her over her shirt.

"I love watching you move for me. You feel so fucking good in my hands."

She moaned and swiveled her hips for me while I nipped her lip.

"I'll tell you a secret," I murmured.

"Tell me," she sighed as my hands cupped and massaged her breasts.

Leaning forward I traced the rim of her ear with my tongue. "I'm going to taste every single inch of you, Firefly."

Her gasp was audible as I lifted her shirt off and growled at the sight of her delicate breasts. Wrapping my hands along her soft flesh, her supple tits spilled out right into my mouth. Two perfect dew drops made to be sucked and licked. While I was tasting those delicious buds, I reached between us, undoing the button on her shorts. I couldn't wait any longer, and in this crazy haste, I bit down hard on her tight little nipple. She moaned out loud and lifted her hips enough for my fingers to slip through the opening and down to her silky panty covered core.

I groaned against her. "You like it rough, baby?"

She shook her head, her lips parted in ecstasy. "I don't know how to like it, Ryan. I've never done it before. I just know I like how you're doing it."

I paused for a moment. I didn't even think about the repercussions of this. She was a virgin. Of course, she was. Just knowing that I'd be the first man inside of her had me thrumming in excitement. I'd lost almost everything in my life, and never had I wanted anything more than Cecilia Cepeda. For the first time in my life I was scared of this strong, beautiful woman. If she only knew-I'd never needed anyone as much as I needed her.

I felt her fingers run through my hair, her soft touch melting my heart. "It's okay, baby. I want you to."

"So easy for you isn't it?"

"It's not easy at all," her husky whisper turned into a moan as she moved beneath me, my hard cock pressing into the juncture between her thighs. "Take it out. Please."

"Fuck," I reach down and in seconds I had my pants and briefs down at my knees. Sliding her shorts down her well-toned legs, I groaned at the sight of her. The feel of her pussy on the head of my dick made me shudder. I looked down and my cock jumped at the sight of my precum coating her lips, leaving traces along the golden curls.

"Fuck, baby."

She clung to me, her hands running up my shoulders while her legs spread wide for me. "Do it, Ryan. I'm ready."

My eyes met hers and gently I inserted myself inside of her. I bit my lip as my overexcited cock slid into the tightest, wettest slit it's ever had.

Don't cum, asshole.

I clenched my eyes shut, enjoying how her pussy opened for me, allowing me to penetrate her. I felt the barrier and her whimper made me hold her tight. Her breath caught as I pushed myself inside of her, breaking her walls. She flinched, her breath hitched, and her head jerked to the side. Biting her lip she clenched her eyes shut and I knew it had stung. Her pussy throbbed around me, and I remained still, careful not to hurt her.

I kissed her cheek and she looked up at me. "You alright?"

She nodded and slowly I began to slide out of her, then slide back in. Gently at first, then faster as she arched her back and cried out for me. She clenched onto my dick so hard it stole my breath. Having her wrapped around me, our hips rocking against each other in a slow erotic dance, it was fucking heaven.

I looked down between us and I could make out the sight of blood tainting my cock, it was a feral instinct to thrust into her harder, rougher. Her nails dug into my biceps and the pain felt good. Her legs spread for me, and as she relaxed, the sound of her wet juices made me respond to her.

I reached between us and she stifled a scream while I took my time rubbing her tight little clit. Her thighs shook, telling me how good I made her feel, while I focused on her. It was better than focusing on my dick which wanted to explode. I watched as her breaths became ragged whispers of pleas I didn't quite make out. Her fingers dug into the dirt at her sides as she arched back, those pretty breasts bouncing seductively as I fucked her. I bent my head down and gave one a little lick. Her moan was pure sin as she dragged me back down and ran her tongue along my own. Her kiss was innocently sexy, her breaths getting lost in mine. She cried out as I slammed my cock deep inside of her and the cry turned into a moan as I cradled her ass and grinded my groin against her clit. Our sex was hot and needy.

"Fuck me," she whispered, her head flung back as I grabbed her hips and gave her what she asked for. Her pleas now loud enough for me to hear.

"Fuck me! Please, Ryan! Shit, that feels so fucking good. Yes!"

I smirked as my cock pulsed inside of her, I liked giving her this. Turning her into my own personal slut. "Such a dirty little mouth. I'll put it to good use one of these days. Make it lick my cock."

She moaned and gasped as I dragged my cock out of her, teasing her with the tip before ramming back into her. "What? You like to think of sucking my dick." I leaned over her, my lips on hers. "You want to taste my cream, Angel?"

She pressed her forehead to mine and the pretty little girl bit her lip and purred. I leaked into her as she placed her feet down on the grass and lifted up to meet my thrusts. It was a frenzy I'd never forget. All I could do was stop and watch as she fucked my cock with her tight virgin pussy. So damn inexperienced in her urgency.

I gave her a smile as I took over, my thumb circling her clit as our bodies grinded and fucked each other. I could feel her cunny wrap around my cock, the sweetest pussy I'd ever felt was about to cum all over me. With a shout, she lifted, her legs shaking while she held her breath. The flush of her cheeks matched that of her breasts, and she came hard on me. Digging at the dirt as her body lifted into mine. I wrapped my arms around her, bringing her up to her knees as my cock exploded inside of her. That aching pulse and relief of my balls emptying out into the prettiest pussy.

"You're fucking perfection, my sweet Firefly."

She cried out as she felt my release, moaning in my ear while she held me tight. I stroked her back as we rocked on our knees, our hearts beating in rhythm. She turned her head and lay it on my shoulder, her warm breath on my cheek.

"I love you, Ryan."

That soft whisper did shit to me. She'd just fucking claimed me, and I didn't give a fuck because I loved her too. I'd never loved anyone so entirely. She was my person and I intended to keep her. Kissing her softly, I just held her, buried deep inside of her as I whispered sweet promises into her ear. Promises I would later realize, I wouldn't be able to keep.

4

RYAN

Six Years Ago...

Carlos *La Plaga* Trejo sat to the right-hand side of *La Muerte* at a table in the middle of the clubhouse. Death and the Plague had found each other, and they were a murderous duo. Carlos was a childhood friend of Mario's from Ecuador. He had been recently released from San Quentin and surprise, surprise, he landed on our doorstep. Rumor was he'd murdered his own father because he dumped his cocaine stash down the toilet. Put a bullet in his head and then waited for the cops to come get him while sitting on the couch watching TV, all while his father lay a few feet away from him. The loss had cost him millions, and when it went to trial he pleaded self-defense. He was let out for good behavior. Then again, who hasn't committed murder or some degree of felony in the Death Row Shooters. We had every kind of malignant disease roaming the club.

The Death Row Shooters now had a new identity, that

of murderers and thieves. If you owed them money, you better pay back quick or they'd have your head, and these fuckers were brutal. The were the type to leave you to bleed, guts out, on your mother's doorstep, so she'd find you the next morning. At times they'd even send you in parts, promising the family would be next if they didn't pay up. As soon as they had the money, they'd bury you out back along with all the other dumb fucks that thought they could get away with it. A debt owed to the Death Row Shooters, was like owing the devil your soul, and they'd take their payment one way or another. They were a bunch of hot heads who didn't respect life, not even their own.

I was behind the bar tonight keeping watch. There was one rat I had in my sights. One who had his eyes set on what was mine. Everyone was aware that my Firefly had grown up to be a beautiful woman. Eighteen years old and she had filled out in all the right places. I couldn't help but gawk at her, and glare at any fucker who even thought about her in the wrong way. Unfortunately for this one, he didn't seem to understand she was taken. And she was, even if I hadn't been vocal about it. Didn't really see the need to since she was with me constantly. And just a few days ago she'd become a part of me. When she wasn't around, I missed the fuck out of her. I promised her that night that I would always be here for her, that I'd never leave her side, and I meant every goddamn word.

I slammed down the glass on the bar top and startled, Poe looked up at me. "What the hell are you doin' man?"

"What the fuck are *we* doing?"

Poe raised a brow, knowing what was coming. It was the same tirade over and over again, but no one seemed to listen to me. "We need to get the fuck out of here."

"You know we don't go anywhere without Simon.

Unless he moves, we move, and he ain't leavin' this place. He built this bar up with Nate, made it his home." Poe leaned in and slammed his finger on the bar top for emphasis as he spoke. "And no fucking delinquents are gonna take it from him."

"Then we need to do something. We're living on edge here. They might hurt her," my eyes flew to Cecilia who looked agitated as her father called her over.

"I can't see her like this, Brother. She should be in college, far away and out of this fucking hell hole."

"She's not leavin' without you. And you ain't leavin' without Simon. It's a fucking vicious circle that keeps sucking you in."

He was right. I was twenty-one and old enough to take Cecilia and leave, but I couldn't turn my back on Simon. And I had a debt that I needed to claim from La Muerte. I wouldn't stop until I saw him six feet under, or well behind bars. I preferred to watch the maggots seep from his eyes. He would pay for the light he took that day, the innocence that he kept darkening day after day with his ugliness and vile shit. I was angry, and my fury only simmered until eventually it would explode.

"You see the two new members these fucktards brought in?"

Poe nodded while taking a long pull of his beer. "I saw them."

"One's a fucking rapist, the other is a cold-blooded killer. What the fuck do you think they're gonna do to that pretty girl?"

"What I think you need to do is calm the fuck down before you get a bullet put through that thick skull of yours."

"Cecilia! Ven aca!" Mario called her over and she glanced at me, that pleading look in her eye again.

I'm right here baby girl.

I clutched the rag in my hand and kept my eyes on her as she made her way around the tables towards her father. La Plaga's leery eyes never left her body and I had a strong urge settle in me to rip them out of his skull. He called himself her Uncle, but I was fully aware of the disgusting perversions he wanted to do to her. He wasn't quiet about it either. Always venting that he'd take her for a ride when she least expected it. I'd clench my jaw and keep walking, but he had no clue I had a bullet engraved with his initials on it. I kept it in my pocket as a reminder that I wasn't a good man. That I was a Death Row Shooter. That I feared nothing, especially when it came to the safety of my girl.

As Cecilia approached their table, I was on alert. I watched as her father clutched at her apron bringing her forward while he played with the hem of her skirt. The motherfucker to his right chuckled and tugged her onto his lap, dirty hands coming around her waist. She squirmed, and I could see the panic in her eyes, but the fucker didn't let her go. I snapped in that moment, and if it wasn't for Ash who placed his hand on my shoulder and held me back, there was going to be a full out shootout in the Death Row Shooters clubhouse. I had a hand on my gun which I kept beneath the bar top in case of moments like these.

"Keep it cool and steady, Turner. You don't want to start shit you can't finish."

"Oh, I'm planning to finish it." I ground my teeth while I watched Cecilia squirm on La Plaga's lap. The more she struggled, the more he seemed to enjoy himself. Meanwhile her father had placed his hand on her knee and was rubbing her thigh trying to soothe her.

"So, you like big bad bikers, huh?" La Plaga licked her cheek while his hand roamed to her breast.

"Let her go!" I yelled out grabbing my gun and pointing it right at his head.

"Come on Turner, I just want to have a little taste of her. A good Club Officer shares with his brothers?"

"She's not to be shared with anyone! And you are far from being my brother."

"Fuck my life," Ash exhale behind me and then I felt him at my side, gun drawn and pointed at La Muerte.

"Let her go, Carlos. This kid ain't playing around. Rules are rules and they're to be followed. You got his woman in your hands there."

Carlos smirked. "Cecilia is mine, by blood. I can do whatever the fuck I want to her." With that said he stuffed his hand between her legs and my finger twitched on the trigger while she gasped and struggled to get out of his grasp.

"And I don't follow rules," La Plaga's thick accent made my blood run cold. "I break every fucking rule, and when I'm done, I'll break every single bone in your brother's body. But right before, I'll let him watch as I take her pretty little pussy."

His raised the hem of her skirt, his hand replacing La Muerte's hand and sliding it along her white silk panties. Tears came down her cheeks as she kicked at them, but Carlos held her down.

I placed my hand on the trigger, ready to blow his fucking head off if I had to. He wrapped himself tighter around Cecilia and my blood blazed. "I said let her go."

"After I give her a nice little ride on my cock." He lifted a strand of her hair off her shoulder, running his hand down her arm. She flinched, tearing her eyes away.

"She doesn't want to be touched," I took a step forward, but Ash placed a hand on my shoulder.

"Easy, Ryan." I looked over at him and he signaled for me to look to my left. Three of the members had taken their guns out and the barrels were all pointed at me.

"We're just going to have a little fun with her. We won't hurt your- how do you call her- ahhh yes," he pressed his lips to her ear and smiled at me. "Firefly."

I was ready to murder every single fucker in this place when the doors to the bar slammed opened and in walked four of the toughest bikers I'd ever met. Everyone turned and the club went silent. Wolf Stone, Grayson Carter, Derek Matheson, also known as Bear, and Cain Scardino, the Hellbound Lovers Sargeant at Arms. They were like bulls entering the stadium and they saw red when they spotted Mario.

Mario turned pale, he looked back at Carlos and then turned to Wolf. La Plaga snarled and released Cecilia. "I'm not done with her yet!" He pointed at me and took his place near Mario as the Hellbound Lovers bounded through the entry.

As soon as he released her, she ran to my side, gripping my hand. Securing a hold around her waist I pulled her behind the bar and whispered for her to stay hidden in the back. I knew this visit wasn't going to be a friendly one, and the last thing I wanted is to worry about her getting hurt. It wasn't the Hellbound Lovers style to shoot up a place, but money could turn the most honest of men into evil bastards.

Wolf had been announced the new President of the HLMC just a few months ago after he got back from wherever the fuck he'd been sent to during the war. Ex-navy seal or something. He was said to be a callous son of a bitch, but

I had great respect for him. Any man who could walk into a room and command like he did, deserved my respect.

His eyes narrowed in on the bunch and I caught a few of the cowards stir in their seats. The thing about the Hell-bound Lovers MC is that they were the type of club you wanted on your side. Being on their bad side would get you killed. They were good men, but they'd been known to lay down the law every once and a while. They did it once with the Devil's Syndicate, and they'd do it again if they had to. Nick, the co-founder of the HLMC had been good with friends with Nate. He had a warm destitution towards Simon. At Nate's funeral, Ryder Chase, his second in command, who'd also passed away a few years back, had offered Simon to be patched over if he wanted it. Last I heard, the offer still stood.

"Mario! Just the person I wanted to see." Wolf walked in and shifted over to our side of the bar, nodding at us.

"Hey fellas," he uttered softly. He has that about him. He didn't need to shout or act up to be intimidating. I heard he learned that out there in the desert. He'd come back with that look in his eye. The look that said he'd killed over a hundred men and he wouldn't hesitate to kill one more if he had to. Not a lot of men liked to cross Wolf's path, especially with that rumor going around that he used to torture people. You never knew what was going on in that head of his.

"Hey Ryan. Where's your cos?"

"Went out on a job. Should be back soon."

Wolf nodded and leaned back on the counter. All activity had stopped as they watched him, and I opened a beer and slid it over to him. He didn't even flinch as he gripped the bottleneck and gulped it down.

"Good beer," he stated as he set the half empty bottle

down on the bar top and wiped his mouth. I knew he was being sarcastic since the Hellbound Lovers were the ones who supplied our alcohol.

"You gotta nice place here, Mario." He took a good look at his surroundings. "Real nice. Lots of space." His comment implied he was interested in the property. As if Mario had put up our home as collateral and the Hellbound Lovers had come in to collect a debt.

"It is a nice space. My space," he replied opening his arms wide, with a smug smile on his face. His missing tooth creating a gap on the right corner. He was one ugly motherfucker.

"What brings the Hellbound Lovers round these parts? You're a little far off your territory."

The high-pitched screeching of a chair as it scraped against the floorboards made everyone turn towards the sound. Bear took a seat in a corner and crossed his legs up on the table. Grayson, the Hellbound Lovers new VP, pulled a chair out as well, smirking as he took a seat. Like I said, these guys didn't play. When they showed up it meant shit was going down.

"Looks like you haven't been very hospitable to Cain here, Mario." Grayson pointed at the man by the doorway. He was a big man, mean looking. I'd met Cain once or twice, mostly when he came by to claim payment for the dealings we had with them. If he'd brought reinforcements this time around, it didn't look good on the clubhouse.

"He hasn't received a response from you on payment yet. So we figured we'd come over and give you a little reminder."

Mario looked nervous as Wolf played with a bullet he'd just pulled out of his pocket. His eyes only focused on the bullet, yet the whole fucking club was focused on him. Mario began to stutter.

"Uh, well...yeah. I was going to answer him."

"You owe us five grand for the liquor, five hundred for shipping it over. Plus, any fees for us coming over here to...*talk* shit out."

"Y-yes." He turned to La Plaga and whispered in his ear. The fucker looked over at Wolf with hatred in his eyes, but Wolf just smirked at him and shrugged. He turned and went off to find the money.

Cain paced the entrance like a Lion in his den, a rifle pressed to his side. Everyone just kind of watched him carefully. Every single man was on edge. One wrong move and I knew the Death Row Shooters were dead. Wolf knew his kin, which is why he moved over to our side, his back to me. If something did go down, he knew we would be counted on.

A hush fell over the clubhouse as we waited for Carlos to return with the payment. Simon chose that instant to walk in. Cain lifted his gun, aiming it at his head, but dropped it when he realized who it was.

"Bear!" Simon's smile was big and welcoming as he reached out to the burly and pulling him in for a warm hug. They laughed and pounded each other's backs like old friends would. After Ryder died, they'd formed a strong bond. My cousin knew what it meant to lose your family, and so did Bear, they'd formed a tight kinship.

"What the hell are you doing here, brothers?" He nodded at Grayson and Wolf in acknowledgement.

Bear frowned and shook his head. "Just getting payment on a small debt that your Prez here owes us."

Simon narrowed his eyes on Mario. "I hope all is good

with the money, *Prez*," the emphasis on the title dripped with hatred.

"We're working on it. It's none of your goddamn business, anyway."

"Not mine, but it is Pooch's over there. I mean he is the club Treasurer."

Pooch raised his eyes and blinked twice. He was a good kid but had no clue what it meant to run a club, let alone deal with the money coming in. I hated that he was associated with Mario, his nephew and Cecilia's cousin. He was too easily influenced by his Uncle and the rest of them to let me get into his head. But the kid listened every once in a while, he wasn't stupid.

"Pooch does what I tell him to do."

Wolf took a step forward and I could see that the silence in the room became heavier as Simon continued to challenge him. "Well then, what the fuck do we have him for? If you tell him what to do, how are we supposed to trust our money is taken care of?"

Carlos walked in at that moment, slamming a wad of cash on the table in front of Grayson. Simon turned to him, fury in his eyes. Wherever he'd just gone, some bad shit had gone down, and Simon wasn't backing down. He was instigating.

"The money is taken care of." La Plaga took his stance at the center of the room eyeing Simon, but we all knew that was a wrong move.

"You wanna' tell me motherfucker why I was just chased down Folsom fucking Boulevard by some crazy ass sons of bitches who said you sent them?"

"I don't know what the fuck you are talking about. You're always talking crazy shit."

Simon lunged forward and was stopped by Wolf, who

placed a hand on his chest. "Let it go, Turner. I'll look into it."

Simon looked down for a minute, clenching his fists and jaw. I could tell he wasn't happy, and he was trying his best to control himself.

"He tried to get me killed. If it wasn't for the Devil's Syndicate who showed up out of nowhere, I'd be fucking dead," he uttered beneath his breath. I hopped over the bar and came up to him.

"You alright?"

He looked at me for a long moment and placed a hand on my shoulder. He leaned in and spoke just loud enough for me and Wolf to hear. "If something happens to me, you take that girl of yours and you run, you hear me."

I shook my head, dread now looming over my head. "Nothing's gonna happen to you."

"You just do as I say," he gripped the nape of my neck and pressed his forehead to mine. "Swear to me you'll do as I say."

I nodded. "I swear it."

"Good man," he patted my cheek and turned to Wolf. An unspoken understanding between them. Looking back at Bear, he smiled.

"I hope you got what you came for, old friend. Make sure we don't owe you anything."

Bear looked at him, worry furrowing his brow. "I got it. But you let me know if you need anything. I promised Nate you had my full protection. Anyone touches a hair on your head, they answer to the Hellbound Lovers. That goes for your family there too and anyone who is your kin."

Simon nodded. He knew what that meant. The Hellbound Lovers had just offered protection and they had done it on purpose so that everybody heard. We were under the

HLMC shadow now, which meant if anyone fucked with us, they'd hunt them down and kill them. That was an unwritten law, one that was rarely challenged. I could tell Simon was grateful, and God help me, so was I.

Wolf patted my back and put a hand over my shoulder. "Now that the debt is settled. I got somethin' for you kid. Courtesy of yours truly."

I looked at Simon and he only nodded. "Go on."

Grayson thanked La Plaga for his services and laughed as the fucker cursed under his breath. "I hope I don't have to see your ugly mug again, Muerte. It won't be such a pleasant visit next time."

"Fuck you!" Mario cursed and the lot of them laughed while I walked out with the Hellbound Lovers. For some reason, leaving Simon alone didn't sit well with me.

As soon as Wolf had me outside, he turned me over to Bear who placed his hand on my shoulder. "If you need anything, don't hesitate to ask us kid. You understand."

"Yes, Sir."

"Simon asked me to bring this for you," he handed me a key, a Hellbound Lovers patch engraved on a silver keychain. He backed up and pointed to the shiny black Harley parked in the alleyway. "This is yours. Technically Simon's but he wanted you to have it. He did a job for us a few weeks back and we wanted to bring the payment over. It's a good baby, take care of her."

"Are you shittin' me?" I ran over to the bike, excitement in my bones. I was dying to have a bike and Simon knew it.

"We were going to bring it by anyway, had spoken to Simon a few days ago. He told us you just turned twenty-one."

"He sounded like a proud dad," Wolf chuckled.

I smiled as I stroked the leather seating. "Sit, try her out," Grayson came over.

I slid into the seat and revved her up, loving the sound of the engine when it roared to life. Fuck, this was my bike. Mine. I'd never been given anything in my life, and here I was receiving a second gift, the first was the leather bracelet secured around my wrist. I took a second to grasp this when I felt Wolf walk up beside me.

"You need anything, you know where to find us."

I nodded, gulping down the knot in my throat. I wanted to ask if they'd take me with them, if I could join their brotherhood, but I looked back at the bar and remembered who was inside. I couldn't leave. I had too many people who counted on me in there.

I watched as Bear hopped into the chase vehicle they'd brought, Wolf's black pickup truck. Grayson and Cain revved up their bikes and their engines roared to life, filling the silence as they took off. My only thought was how badass they were, how they didn't have a threat over their head on a constant basis. I wanted to live like them, and in a way, I was envious and angry that I had to watch my back every second of every day. Their lights disappeared in the distance leaving me in the dim silence once again. I was concentrated on the bike when the sound of a bullet being fired pierced the quiet of the night. My eyes shot up, and dread swept over me, telling me things weren't going to be the same again.

5

RYAN

That night- Six Years ago...

The bike toppled over in my rush to get in through the doors. It was long forgotten as I tugged my gun out of the waistband of my jeans. It nearly slipped from my fingers when I walked in, stopping short at the sight before me. Both Ash and Poe were on their knees, guns pointed at their temples. Standing just a few feet before them was Simon, La Muerte's gun pointed to his head.

"Kneel," Mario uttered, but Simon refused, spitting at his feet.

"Always going against me! Eres un traidor de mierda!"

"I will never kneel to you," Simon growled.

Mario took a step back and grinned. "Then I'll just have to make you."

As the door slammed shut behind me everything went still. Simon turned to look at me, an apology carved in his eyes, and suddenly there was the blast of a bullet being fired. Simon's head snapped back as blood splattered out of his temple and he fell to his knees first, before slowly crumpling to the floor.

"Nooo!" My eyes focused on his limp body and suddenly everything in my body went deadly still. I let the darkness consume me as I raised the Glock in my hand. After a moment's pause, as if in slow motion, I started to fire.

Bam. Bam. Bam. Bam.

One right after the other, as if I were in target practice. First the two holding my brothers captive, the one in the back who had taken out a rifle, the one to the right of me who thought he was faster than I was. Out of the corner of my eye I spotted Ash and Poe slide across the floor, shots began to fire around me. The steel barrel of La Muerte's gun turned to me, staring me in the eyes. I cocked my head and we both fired at the same time. His shot whizzed by my temple, while mine hit him right in the center of his ugly face. Right through his cheek. He stumbled back, and I followed him as he lay on the floor, squirming and squealing like the rat that he was.

I stood over him, his wide black eyes on me. "You thought you'd win? You thought you could take everything I had and you wouldn't pay? I want you to remember my face before I take your miserable fucking life and know, that I was the one who took over. I was the one who sent you back to hell."

I cocked the gun and fired two shots into his head. I spit in his bloodied face and turned to find Cecilia crouched down low on the side of the bar. Her big eyes watching me, shock penetrating through them.

Fuck my life!

I flew across the bar towards her only to be tackled by one of the opposing members. He was a big guy, went by the name of Morgue. He wanted to be like me, the asshole. But he was an arrogant motherfucker and couldn't match up to me in any fight. I was an agile son of a bitch, and he was a big tub of lard that didn't know when to give up. A piece of shit who shot people dead just for pronouncing his name wrong. I fucking hated the bastard.

With a right hook I sent him down to the ground, cocking my gun I shot him twice. One in the chest, one in the head. Fucker didn't even have a chance.

"Ryan watch out!" Ash's shout made me turn, and sure enough, Pooch was standing behind me-the hand holding his gun was shaking real bad. If I wasn't careful, he'd scare, and I'd get a hole through me.

"Pooch think this through. You don't want to do this."

"Y-you killed my family." I knew how he felt. I'd just lost all of mine.

Nodding, I tilted the gun slightly as I spoke. It was as if somebody else had taken me over, the gun becoming a part of me. "You could say that, but I don't want to kill you. You're a good kid Pooch. I can give you a family here if you give me a chance."

His eyes focused on movement behind me and I saw Cecilia shift. "Eyes up here, Pooch. She's under my protection, nothing's gonna happen to her."

"How do I know that?"

"Because I'm giving you my word. And out of all these fuckers you know my word means gold."

We stood there, guns pointed at each other, one hand trembling, the other steady and lethal. If I made any sudden movement, he'd snap. "Come on, Pooch. Make the choice."

He looked down for a second and slowly began lowering his gun. "Cobarde," the sound of La Plaga's voice echoed from my right and the bullet hit Pooch square in the chest.

"Motherfucker!" I yelled as I emptied my gun in his direction. The fucker was fast, and he tackled me around the waist, slamming us into tables that broke beneath our weight. He was a heavy-set guy, and it felt like a ton of bricks had taken my breath away. He was incessant in his blows and I wound up trying to fight him off me, curling up and trying not to get hit in the sides anymore. The blows were heavy, and I knew I was going to lose a few ribs. Suddenly, someone lifted him off me and I was able to get in a gulp of breath.

A quick blow to the head and the fucker stumbled back. Poe lifted him and rained down on him, one punch after the other. Letting him go, he dropped to the floor. He fumbled back towards the door and suddenly a shot rang out sending Poet back a few steps. I watched terrified as my friend fell to his knees, but before the other member could put a shot in him, Ash got to him first, bullets imploding in his chest and bringing him down. I grabbed at Poe and dragged him towards the back of the bar. The bullet went clean through the shoulder, but he'd survive. Grabbing the rag on top of the bar I pressed it to his wound. I looked back at Cecilia and managed to stagger back up. I took the bullet out of my pocket and slid it in the chamber.

"I'll come back for her, Turner! Mark my fucking words, maricón! I'll come back and I'll ruin you!"

I aimed the gun at La Plaga who was just about to reach the door, when Ash pulled me aside. "Go!"

"Get out of my way!" I struggled to get loose but Ash had a strong grip on me.

He shook me hard and my eyes finally met his. "Take her and fucking go. I'll take care of him! Go!"

I looked down at Cecilia who was only a few feet away from me. Tears slid down her cheeks and she shook in fear. I had to choose. Cecilia or La Plaga.

"I've got him! Go!" Ash yelled at me again as he ran towards the door where Carlos had escaped through. I knew I had to trust him. Turning, I looked at Poe who was slumped on his side. He took his gun out and cocked the trigger while he signaled for me to go. I lifted her up into my arms and ran towards the side door. Stepping out, I spotted the Harley tipped on its side.

"Fuck," I muttered. "I'm gonna set you down baby girl. Just for a minute." She nodded, and I settled her on the ground, her legs shaky but she was able to wait for me as I lifted the bike and started it up.

"Let's go!"

Taking a quick look back at the bar, she took a deep breath and slid onto the back seat. Pressing her cheek to my back she held on tight. She felt so damn good I almost forgot what I was doing. The scent of vanilla swept into my senses and I gripped her hands as I backed out. Patting her knee, I revved up the engine and took off. I knew exactly where I had to go. They had offered protection and I was taking it.

We ran into the Hellbound Lovers' clubhouse, and I ran right into Cain. "Whoa! Hold on there." He gripped me by my jacket and looked me over. I must have looked like a bloodied mess cause he sat me down and got me a shot of whiskey. Cecilia hovered close to me, and I dragged a seat over and had her sit down next to me.

"What are we doing here?" She asked, looking around the old dive bar. The Hellbound Lovers had a property further North that Nick, the ex-founder had converted into a diner after Ryder passed away. It had been Devil's Syndicate property at one time, but the Hellbound Lovers had bought it fair and square and the DSMC had been pissed for a long time. When Regina Thorn and Ryder Chase became an item, everything simmered down. After that whole mess and Wolf taking over a new Chapter, they'd acquired this old place, which by the looks of it was being remodeled.

"It's okay. These are good men. They ride under one of the most honorable codes. They offered us protection."

She gripped my hand and pressed herself to my side as Wolf returned with Grayson. I swear, the guy looked meaner every time I saw him. Not really the type I wanted around Cecilia, especially the way she was shaking at my side. Wolf slid a glass a water to her but then turned to me.

"What happened?"

"Why'd the fuck you bring him?" I signaled at Grayson without looking at him.

Wolf tilted his head towards the man. "He's my VP. Wherever I go he goes."

I nodded. "Can I trust him?"

"If I can trust him, you can trust him."

"Where's Bear?" I looked around wanting to see a friendly face.

"Bear's out on a job. Look kid, if you don't trust me, I can't help you. Just tell me what happened?"

"Simon's dead," I whispered. "I put a bullet in La Muerte's head and there was a shootout at the bar."

Wolf remained emotionless, an eerie calm in his glare. "How many dead?"

I shrugged. "I don't remember-nine, eleven tops."

Grayson mumbled something in Wolf's ear, and he

acknowledged it and turned to Cecilia. "You okay, sweetheart? You want somethin' to eat?"

She shook her head and snuggled closer to me, practically wrapping herself around my arm. I knew that this was not going to be good for either of us, but I had to do it.

"La Plaga is out there somewhere. Ash is looking for him. I can't leave her alone and I can't take her with me. He swore he'd come back for her. I need protection for her."

Wolf nodded and looked at Grayson. They spoke in silence and it fucking grated on my nerves. "How long until Bear gets back?"

"Look kid, we're it. You're gonna have to deal with us or go somewhere else."

I nodded. "Yeah, sorry. I'm a little on edge."

The door banged open and a member walked in. Cecilia jumped beside me, and I tensed. The guy paused, looking over at us, then nodded at Wolf and kept walking. I turned back to the men and frowned. "Can you help us?"

"You know what happens when you ask for the Hellbound Lovers help?"

"She becomes your property. I know."

"What?" She whispered beside me. I looked over at her and then at Wolf. "Can you give us a sec?"

He nodded. "You're safe here. Take your time."

As soon as they walked away, I turned to Cecilia and grabbed her hands. "You heard what he said. La Plaga will come after you. You didn't see it, but I saw it in his eyes. If he gets a hold of you, he'll hurt you, kill you. These men are good men, they'll protect you."

"What about you?"

"Don't worry about me. But I have to go back. I need to make sure my brothers are okay. I can't live with myself if they're not, and I won't stop until I know La Plaga is buried next to that piece of shit," my blood boiled as I thought of La Muerte. "But I can't do any of that if you are not okay. I need to know you're safe."

"What will they do to me?"

"I don't know. But their known to offer protection. They're good for it, trust me."

"I don't know, Ryan. Can't I just go with you? I can hide somewhere until you're done."

I cupped her cheeks and brought her face up, so I was looking into her eyes. "You know I love you, right?"

She closed her eyes and tears swept down her cheeks. "I love you too."

Hearing those words made my heart soar, but I shoved the feeling aside, forcing myself to focus on what I had to do. "I'll come back for you, baby, and we'll be together again."

She gripped my wrists. "You have to promise you'll come back, Ryan. Promise me you'll come back."

I pressed a kiss to her forehead and hugged her tight. "I promise," I whispered, knowing it may be an empty promise at this point. I signaled to Wolf and they returned.

"You ready?"

I shrugged. "Where do I sign."

Grayson handed me a contract with stipulations on it. She was under their protection until they deemed it safe for her to leave their side. She will be removed from the area and secured by the Hellbound Lovers. She became Hellbound Lovers property which meant she would be treated with respect, such as an Ol' Lady would.

"Will I be able to get to her?"

"Do you want to get to her?" Wolf asked grimly.

I shook my head and heard her gasp as I signed her off

to them. "Ryan," she touched my arm but I avoided what I knew was a troubled look.

"It's for the best, Cecilia. Even if they torture me, I'll never give you up because I won't know where you are."

She grabbed my cheek and turned my face to hers. "I swear to God, you better come back in one piece."

I kissed the palm of her hand, looked at Wolf and Grayson, and slowly stood up. "Take care of her Hellbound Lover." I looked at Wolf. "Because if you don't, I will personally come after you."

The man beside me went still. He must have noticed I was dead serious because Wolf nodded, remaining stoic. "You don't need to worry. She'll be left in good hands."

I reached out my hand and he took it, giving it a hard shake. But as I went to pull away, he tugged me forward. "But you threaten me again, and I'll forget we offered *you* protection."

I gulped and nodded. "Understood."

He let go of my hand and I gave Cecilia a gut-wrenched look before I tore myself away and walked out. As soon as the door slammed shut behind me, I screamed out and fell to my knees. Silent tears poured down my face as I knelt beneath that street lamp. Simon's face and Cecilia's sad eyes kept running through my head. The look on Pooch's face as he was shot, looking at me as if asking why I hadn't done anything. And Poe and Ash, how they'd looked so fallen when they realized Simon was gone. I roughly wiped my tears and stood up. Getting back on the bike, the tires squealed on the concrete as I geared it towards the clubhouse. It was our home, and I was taking it back.

6

RYAN

PRESENT DAY...

I STOOD AT THE CLIFF LOOKING OUT AT THE mountainside, Poe was by my side. "did you hear about the docks?"

We'd acquired half the docks through the war between the Hellbound Lovers and the Colombian cartels. It was supposedly our payment for a job well done. A payment I didn't really care for, yet I knew when not to deny a profitable acquisition.

"Do we know who they are?"

"Not yet, Sir. We actually asked a fellow brother for help."

I narrowed my eyes, hidden in my shades. "Riggs?" I had nothing against John Riggs. If anyone was good at finding intel it was him, I just didn't enjoy the Hellbound Lovers knowing my business.

"Next time that happens you ask first before getting other men to babysit our shit for us."

"The shipments are large crates and they've been stationed there for a few days."

"Before we make a move, we watch and do our part to assess the situation. Get Ash to help you on this one."

I looked down at my watch and frowned. "You think they'll show?"

"They have to show, they know what happens if they don't."

"I'm done with this shit, brother. This is the last of it. I don't want any more dealings with the Triads after today. I don't want anyone else hurt with their ruthless bullshit. They don't give a fuck who they take down with them and they have disrespected the Death Row Shooters."

"Jeffries is a smart legal aid. Last time we spoke he said he'd bring the dissolution of contract."

"I'm not signing shit without reading it thoroughly, twice."

Poe nodded. "Agreed."

"These fuckers want to use our resources, they can go kiss my ass. After what happened to Digger the deal is off."

"You got it, Prez."

We'd done business with the Triads in some money laundering deals, but I was done. Digger had gotten shot at last time he went to collect, and the deal was now off. The sound of wheels crunching on gravel caught my attention and, in the distance, I could see the sun bounce off the roof of the Cadis coming our way. Three shiny black cars, stacked one right after the other, parked themselves right behind us. I shifted over to the bikes which were on the side of the road. There was no way in hell I was getting cornered by these fuckers.

The door propped open and out stepped Zhang Wei, one of the leaders of this particular Triad clan. He orchestrated the whole contract in the first place. Jeffries, his legal counsel, stepped out next. He was a smug bastard, tall, blonde hair, expensive suit that he didn't fucking tailor. For some reason, that shit bothered me. A lot. A man who doesn't tailor his suit wasn't to be trusted in my book. If he couldn't take enough care of himself, why the fuck would he give a shit about you.

"Ryan Simon, long time no see. How are you my friend?" Zhang's thick accent always made me feel like I was in an old Kung Fu movie. But this was no movie, and as he approached me, I kept my guard up. Leaning back on the bike, I folded my arms over my chest, making no effort to greet the slime bag.

"Oh, come on, old friend. Don't be like that, it was an honest mistake."

"A mistake that cost you a contract."

"No, no. We have not discussed that yet."

"There is no discussion. Look Mr. Wei, I understand that you run an enterprise, but guess what, so do I. Fuck, so do many people. And the first rule of the game, is don't fuck with the people who feed you. And see," I cleared my throat for emphasis, "you didn't just fuck with some random guy, no." I shook my head and took my glasses off. "You fucked with one of my brothers."

Zhang Wei stared at me, squinting in the sun. "It was a mistake. It won't happen again."

"You're right. It won't. Because we won't be working together again."

"Ryan, please."

"You call me Mr. Simon and show me some respect." The tension in the air rose and I could sense Poe stiffen at my side. "The deal is broken, it's over."

I signaled for Jeffries who looked at his boss, a worried

look in his eye. "The contract Jeffries. We're signing it here, in the middle of nowhere. My man, Poe Chambers, and yourself as witnesses."

Zhang nodded to Jeffries and he reached into his expensive Italian leather briefcase and pulled out the paperwork. I slammed it down on the hood of the Cadillac and read through it, twice. It stipulated that the contract had been fully completed by the Death Row Shooters President, Ryan Simon, and that all transactions, as negotiated, were finalized. A penalty of three million would be deposited into the Death Row Shooters account by twelve noon.

I checked my watch and picked up my phone while staring at Zhang Wei. I flipped it open to view my bank account, and sure enough three million had been deposited. I smiled at Poe and nodded at Lee. "Looks like you're a man of your word."

"Before you do this, know this is not going to go over well with my bosses."

"Yeah well," I raised the pen and signed on the line. "I don't know your bosses."

I slammed the contract into Jeffries chest and reached out a hand to the Triad leader. "It's a shame, Mr. Wei. It was good doing business with you."

He looked at me grimly but shook my hand either way. "I hope this doesn't come back to bite you in the ass."

I slid my glasses back on and gave him a sly grin. "If it does, we'll be ready."

Raising my hand, I did a little wave and hopped onto my bike. Speeding off all I could think was, good riddance. I was done interacting with that shit head. The Triads were bad news and as much as I didn't want to be on their bad side, I knew they'd keep their word. I had too many connections they didn't want to fuck with. One word from me and they'd lose so much money they'd be out on the streets in seconds. That wasn't my intention, but every once in a while, I liked reminding them of what power I was holding over their head.

In the last few years of my Presidency I'd made sure the Death Row Shooters made a name for themselves. We still held some shady connections but it was out of necessity more than fear. These connections put food on our table and brought protection to our door. What is it they say, keep your enemies closer. The Death Row Shooters may no longer be the sordid criminals that used to live within our walls, but we weren't backwoods chumps that didn't know how to play the game. We know the rules a lot better than they did, hell, we'd even put some down ourselves. No one fucked with my name or that of my brothers. You were gambling with your life if you did. Take that as a threat if you want to.

Hell, I want you to.

Ash's bike appeared on the road to my left and he joined us in form soon after. Ash to my right, Poe, right behind him. I'd named Poe my Sargent at Arms and he was always with me whenever I had to make negotiations of this kind. He was my ride or die brother at arms, and he was also the smartest fucker I knew. He'd taught himself law and got some pointers from Scarlett Stone while he'd been stationed at Ravenous. Wolf's wife was a sexy spitfire and smart as fuck. She taught Poe everything he needed to become the Death Row Shooters legal counsel. We needed all his brains after that night.

That night.

There isn't much to say about it. When I'd gotten back to the bar it had been emptied out. Digger and Shotgun, ex-members of Nate's Chapter had been called back in by Ash.

We met up in the hospital where Poe was being looked at by one of the nurse's that worked there. Shotgun had a thing for her and she had a little thing for the big guy as well. We had to be careful the cops weren't being called or we'd have to answer to the law. None of us were really in the mood for that shit. After listening to Ash talk, I assumed the vote would go towards him, and I was okay with that. With anyone other than Mario Cepeda. But when he raised his hand, he called out a name I didn't expect.

"I've never seen you wield a gun like that, Brother. That shit was a part of you. In your blood. My vote's for Ryan."

I was in shock as all their hands raised and right then and there we decided to start a new chapter of the Death Row Shooters. I claimed my VP as Ash Warden, Poe became my Sargeant at Arms, Digger my Club Officer, and Shotgun my Enforcer. The founding members called in more reinforcements, and the club soon grew to twenty strong.

I changed my name shortly after, not on purpose, I just kind of adopted it. All the connections we had were under Simon's name. I looked so much like him people started calling me Simon, new connections called me Ryan, and my enemies started calling me the Reaper. Wherever I was, death followed. I had to admit, I liked the fucking title.

We'd been put through heavy trials, trials that shook us to the core. Gunfights we didn't think we'd survive, drug heists that had gone extremely wrong, and some serious trafficking we'd been caught up in. But one thing was for sure, they always had my back and I had theirs. A few months ago, we had word that La Plaga had come out of hiding. Ash had finally done what he'd sought after that night, and he buried him right off of the Pacific Coast Highway.

After that, I wanted out of the shit hole, which is why I

went seeking Wolf again. I wanted Cecilia back, but I also wanted to redeem the Death Row Shooters' name. Cecilia had always been in the center of it all, but I required leverage, and if the Hellbound Lovers needed our help, we'd be there.

The members didn't understand it at first, but they caught on pretty quickly, a few of them even making brothers for life with the HLMC. I was alright with all of that, it was the incessant meddling in my life that was grating on my nerves.

"You talk to Grayson and Wolf?" Ash asked as we sauntered back into the bar. Poe kept looking back making sure we hadn't been followed.

"Yeah," I muttered.

"What they say?"

"They said they'd ask her."

"You think she'll come back?"

I slammed my helmet on one of the tables and turned to look at him. "I don't give a fuck if she wants to come back or not. I'm bringing her home where she belongs."

"Look, kid," he regretted the words as soon as they slipped out of his mouth.

"You call me that again," I pointed at him.

"Stop acting like one and we won't have any more problems."

"I know what the fuck I'm doing."

"That's what you think." Ash's anger was eminent in his stance. He was lookin' for a fight and I was too frustrated to give into it.

"Argh," I waved at him dismissively and walked down the hallway. "Leave me the fuck alone, Ash." I turned my head slightly, "I don't need a father figure, let alone one that forgot his own kid!"

It was a low blow, knowing it wasn't his fault that he couldn't see his boy. I heard him curse and a table flip as I slammed the door shut behind me. I shook my leather jacket off and threw it on the couch before slumping down in my chair. Propping my elbows on the table I hung my head in my hands.

I hated this feeling of emptiness I kept getting when I thought of her. I needed to see her, needed to feel her again. I looked down at my hands, hating myself. So much blood had seeped into them, so much anger and hate. How could I touch her with these hands? I had to make amends, I had to get shit right before she returned. I had to build her a home, one she'd want to stay in. But there was no time left, she'd have to accept what I could give her for now. My patience was wearing thin. I was never the patient type. Usually when I wanted something I just took it. And I wanted her.

My phone pinged and I took it out my back pocket and flung it onto the desk. Wolf's name caught my eye and I stared at the message for a long moment. I realized then, there really was no time.

Dinah's Diner at eight in the morning tomorrow. Don't be fucking late.

My Angel was coming home.

7

CECILIA

I STARED out the window of Dinah's Diner as I waited for him to arrive. From where the diner sat you could see across the Hollywood Hills, the city of Los Angeles bustling down below beneath the clouds of smog. I hadn't been back to California in a long time and I had to admit, I hadn't missed it.

When Wolf had asked me to come back I'd been hesitant at first. When he told me Ryan wanted to see me, I wanted to stay hidden, to make him suffer the pain I'd been struggling through all these years. I'd finally been able to move on, and just when I thought everything was sliding into place, he comes barging in. After a few days I felt bad. Wolf never did ask me for anything, and I'd felt almost obligated to come. But maybe that was an excuse, maybe I was trying to find a way to get here all along.

So many years waiting to see him. My life was so different up in Washington. After that night, Wolf and Grayson had made sure I'd felt safe. They'd set me up with a place in Tacoma, and in the last few years I had dedicated myself to finishing my degree. They told me I didn't have to worry about anything, but I was never one to rely on others and I quickly found a part time job waitressing. It got me through college where I became a registered nurse. Like I said, things were finally coming together. I had just been offered a job at the nearby hospital when I got the call from Wolf. I had two weeks until I started, and I came down for this one visit.

Just one day.

Just one hour.

"Hey, Firefly."

I was startled out of my thoughts by his deep familiar rumble. Turning, I looked up at the man in question, and he took my breath away. The nickname made my heart skip a beat. I hadn't heard it in years and as much as I didn't want to admit it, I'd missed it. I fought back the tears that threatened to burn my cheeks, swallowed the lump in my throat, and stared at the man who had slid into the seat in front of me.

He'd gotten older, not by much though, he was still a pretty boy, but his features had hardened. A grim expression now lay where his brightness once shined. His clear blue eyes had darkened to a deep cobalt blue and his once short hair was now shoulder length, locks of his dark golden hair fell across his face, hiding him from me. A beard lined his face hiding away that strong jawline of his and giving him a permanently dangerous look.

"You gonna stare at me all day, Firefly?"

"Stop calling me that," I glared at him. He could try to intimidate anyone he wants, but that shit won't work on me and he knows it.

Stormy blue eyes narrowed on me, drawing out a shiver from me. And then he shrugged, as if he didn't give a fuck. Leaning back in his chair he took a good long look at me. His eyes lingered on my face, my lips, running down the slope of my neckline and lingering on my breasts. Everywhere they fell was a caress on my body, and I clenched my jaw trying not to make a sound. The man was a complete contradiction. He was all sharp swagger with his expensive satin slacks and sleek black button-down shirt, yet he proudly wore his black leather jacket with the DRSMC patch on the back. Beneath that money-grubbing shirt there were traces of tattoos that lined his arms, tattoos I'd memorized so long ago and probably some new ones. Money and edge, that was Ryan Turner in a package.

"Why did you call me here, Ryan?"

Leaning forward he folded his hands on the table. I couldn't help but focus on his long fingers and the lingering of a tattoo that peeked from beneath the cuff of his shirt. "Why do you think I called you here?"

We stared at one another, until I squirmed beneath his scrutiny. "I'm not at your beck and call, Ryan. I'm not in the mood for games, nor am I property you could once discard and then decide to come back for. I'm not up for grabs."

"When did you learn to talk so pretty?"

"When I was left to fend for myself," I hissed at him letting my anger coil tightly around us.

He didn't say a word, instead he turned, staring out the window, a look of anguish crossed his features and I yearned to lean forward and touch his cheek. "Six years, Firefly. That's how long I've waited for you."

His eyes met mine, older, yes, but they still made me feel that same fire that had burned in me when I was eighteen. I shuddered as his eyes traced my face, a gentle longing buried deep in that glare.

"All that time I craved this moment," his voice lowered.

"Seeing your pretty face again, witnessing how a room lit up when you smiled."

"Ryan," he held up a hand to stop me.

"Six years, Firefly, and I never stopped thinking of you. Not once."

"I'm a different person now, Ryan. I'm not the same young girl you left behind so long ago. I was weak back then, ignorant to what my father's intents were, ignorant to yours as well. I'm no longer that girl that needs your protection. I left that girl behind. I killed her along with us that night."

He nodded as he stared down at his hands, his lips slightly puckered in that childlike pout of his. I stared down at his hands along with him, for as long as I can remember I loved his hands. Their strength, the way they held me. He shifted and out of the corner of his sleeve I spotted the black leather band. Reaching out, I touched it. His breath hitched at the contact, and his hand coiled into a fist, but he didn't pull away.

"You kept it?"

"Of course, I did."

I ran my hand along his fist and he opened his hand while I traced his fingers. I remember how they felt when they stroked my back. How gentle they were as they cradled my face, the roughness of his fingertips as they caressed my cheek. There wasn't a day that went by that thoughts of him wouldn't plague my mind. In all the years that had passed, no one compared to him, and no one ever would.

But as much as I had missed him, I was not going back to that life. I refused to sacrifice myself or my freedom again. I had a life, a new name, happiness.

"I can't go with you Ryan, you know this."

"Firefl..."

"Stop calling me that!" I whispered harshly. "My name isn't Firefly, it isn't even Cecilia. I go by Lia now. I like Lia, she's free to live her life."

"You can be free with me," his hand curled into a fist right over his heart, then he pounded it against the table. "You either come with me now, or I'll steal you away."

"You can't do that, and you know it. Wolf and Grayson will come after you in a heartbeat."

"I'll take you far away where no one can find us."

"And leave this?" I tapped the Death Row Shooters symbol on his bracelet. "I doubt it."

"Please, Cecilia."

Pain and despair shown in his face and I felt for him, because I knew that feeling all too well. I wasn't sure if I was making the right decision. Doubt always loomed over me, and this time it made me hesitate. Maybe I should stay. Maybe he needed me. But where was he when I needed him? Where was he when I was suffering? I was in this turmoil of confusion, stay or go. But this man, Ryan Turner...Simon...whatever grim name he'd chosen for himself, he was still living in the past, and it hurt me to see it weighing him down. How could a man like this ever make me happy?

"I can't do this, Ryan."

I turned to walk off when his hand closed around my wrist, stopping me. We looked at one another, indecision meeting desperation. And somewhere, caught in the middle of all that uncertainty, there was a deep longing that lingered between us. A longing that was tarnished in sorrow and time wasted.

"Don't go, Firefly. Gimme a chance."

"I came to see how you were. You look really good, Ry." I gave him a sad smile. "But I'm not going back. I can't."

"It's different now, Cecilia. Those men don't exist anymore. Ash buried La Plaga only months ago, he was the last of them. We've made something of ourselves, went back to code."

There was so much to say, so much time that was lost, and so much pain. I stared down at the hand that was now wrapped around mine.

"Blood," I muttered.

His eyes followed mine and he wrenched his hand away. "Necessary blood."

"Too much of it," my voice cracked. "And all because of me."

He dragged me towards him and sat me down, kneeling by my side, his face was level with mine. Those hands I remembered so fondly, finally touching me. I concentrated on my breathing as a sense of safety overwhelmed me when he cradled my face. He was so gentle with me.

"I did what I had to do not just for you, but to protect what was mine. You were not the cause of it all. *He* was the monster. It was their fault."

A tear escaped down my cheek, his beard grazing my soft skin, my breath shaky as his lips met my own in a soft kiss. It was a long-awaited meeting of two souls coming together again. The kiss was deep and slow, he was careful, as if though I were a fragile mare that would run away if he startled me. It was instinct to wrap my arms around him, to let out a sigh as his mouth molded to mine.

It's just a sweet kiss, Lia.

A kiss goodbye.

I pushed him away, my lips still tingling from his touch, but I found my strength and got up. He knelt there, his head hung low, and I looked down at the top of his head and realized that what I needed all along was closure. What he gave me was a glimpse into what could have been, and I needed to stay away from that temptation.

"Goodbye, Ryan."

Grabbing my purse, I left him there, and it took everything in me to leave and not look back.

8

RYAN

I WALKED her out and slid my black aviators on, avoiding the glare of the sun. I didn't want this to happen this way, but she'd given me no choice. The President of the Death Row Shooters doesn't fucking beg, and there I was on my knees with my heart in my hands and she thought she was going to walk out on me. She had another thing coming. I looked over at the man by the SUV, glad I'd decided to bring the Escalade with me.

"Cecilia," I whispered.

She turned to me and as she covered her eyes from the glare of the sun, Mikey, one of the prospects, grabbed her from behind. He wrapped a cloth over her nose and mouth and held her tight as she kicked up. She stared at me, wide-eyed, kicking at Mikey's shins and struggling. He dragged her over to the car, out of sight, and after a couple minutes she relaxed in his arms and I simply winked at her as she slowly drifted off to Neverland. She slipped away and I grabbed her from Mikey. I didn't want anybody's grubby paws on her. Lifting her into my arms I laid her down on the back seat and took a moment to take her in. She was as beautiful as ever. I moved her long golden locks aside and kissed her forehead, just how I'd done that night so long ago.

"Welcome home, baby." I whispered to her before closing the door and sliding into the front seat.

HALF AN HOUR LATER I WAS STANDING IN THE MIDDLE of her bedroom. It had recently been remodeled just for her arrival, and I watched in shock as she practically destroyed it. Her eyes had fluttered open just as I'd laid her down in bed and she struggled and screamed until she fought me off her. I'd asked everyone to leave and turned to my fiery tempered vixen. Those gorgeous breasts of hers heaved sexily, her hair rumpled as if she'd just gotten up from a night of wild sex, and her eyes looked half glassed over, probably from the chloroform that hadn't really fucking worked. I should have never trusted Digger. Her scream of frustration startled me as she continued to knock things down, she flung a lamp in my direction and I ducked down, barely dodging it.

"Are you through destroying the room? I thought you'd like to come down for dinner, but..."

"You cannot keep me here!"

"Watch me," I turned to her and she met my gaze head on. She was a fearless little thing, I never thought she'd had this fire in her. She'd definitely changed since last I saw her. I couldn't blame her.

"I don't want to hurt you, Cecilia. It's the last thing I want. But I want you to live and I want you to live by my side. I want you to be free."

"I was free," her voice cracked as tears slid down her

cheeks. "The Hellbound Lovers gave me that freedom and now you're taking it away!"

Her tears tore at my heart, but she needed to understand that there was no freedom without me. I was it or there was nothing. Coming up to her I cupped her cheeks, lifting her head until her shining blue eyes met mine.

"I gave you that freedom! Me! *I* am your freedom. I am your peace. I am your everything. And you'll always be mine. I've been waiting for you, my sweet Cecilia. I've thought of you every day since I left your side. I've missed you more than you could ever imagine. Patiently waiting while the Hellbound Lovers kept you away from me. Not knowing where you were-how you were."

She pulled away from me, brushing roughly at her cheeks. She faced me, her anger boring through me. "That was your fault! You wanted this! I begged you to take me with you and now you want to come back, for what Ryan? To destroy my life once again?"

"That's not why I'm here." I tried grabbing her, but she jerked away from me.

"Don't touch me. I hate you!"

"Hate me if you have to, Firefly. But I'm not letting you go."

"I was happy! I am happy. I want to go back. Take me back, Ryan."

I shook my head. "I can't do that, Cecilia. Forgive me. But I just can't."

I turned away and walked towards the door, stopping short just before opening it. "I just want you to understand that this is more than you and I, Cecilia." I stared back at her fixedly, my heart in my throat as I said the next few words. "This is what my love for you has driven me to, it's all for *you*."

"Love? What do you know about love!" She yelled at me as giant drops of tears escaped down her rosy cheeks.

"It's been six years! You left me six years ago and now suddenly you decide you want me back!" She laughed sarcastically, and irritation flooded through me.

"I waited for you too, Ryan... whatever the hell your last name is." She waved her hand in the air and I found her reaction somewhat amusing.

"I waited so long for you there were nights I couldn't breathe. I'd cry every night, not that you gave a shit. You never cared enough, did you?" She looked down at her hands. "I forgot what it meant to live, Ryan. And when I finally realized you weren't coming, I nearly slit my wrists."

"No," I shook my head, gripping at her wrists, checking for marks.

"I didn't. But you might as well have buried me beside my father."

"Don't fucking say that!" I ran my hands through my hair, desperation ran through me as I stumbled away from her.

"You did that. If it wasn't for Wolf and Grayson, and Scarlett, I'd be dead by now."

"You think I didn't fucking suffer!" I pounded my chest, anguish scarring my soul. "You think I didn't think about you every fucking day, curse myself for leaving you. I'm fucking broken!"

"If you knew what broken meant you wouldn't have done this to me."

"How could you say that to me?"

I was so fucking upset that she hadn't considered me, not even a little bit. That she thought I didn't have a heart. Grabbing her hand, I pressed it to my chest. "This shit beats you know. It fucking breaks too!"

I searched her face while she avoided my eyes. She tried to pull back, but I gripped her wrist and held her hand pressed above my heart. "Don't ever fucking think I wasn't breaking for you," I gritted angrily.

Her eyes met mine and we stood there, seething at one another. I couldn't help but notice how she'd matured, taken on a womanly air that tightened my loins for her. I fucking wanted her with every fiber of being. "You want to take your life for this shit. Do it. And I'll bury you. But your grave will be next to mine. Six feet below this goddamn place."

"You're crazy!"

"Damn fucking straight I am. I am not the boy that left you that night. I'm the man who promised I'd return for you. I kept my fucking promise and now you want to shit on that. You've got a lot to learn little girl if you think I'm gonna let you tear my heart out and stomp on it. You want to know what pain is? Live in my fucking shoes for the last six years and you'll know what it means to suffocate in blood, in battle, in me!"

"Ryan! Ryan!" She yelled as I slammed the door shut behind me and locked it. She wanted to act this way, like a fucking child, then I couldn't trust her, and I'd keep her here until she learned that there was no leaving the Reaper. He had his eyes on her soul, and the only way of escape was through death, both hers and mine.

9

CECILIA

Before I could react, he reached for the door, looked back at me, those damn eyes condemning me as he slammed it shut. When I heard the lock turn I realized what he'd done. Running to the door, I tried to open it, but it wouldn't budge.

"Ryan! Ryan goddamn you!" I slammed my fists on the heavy door frame, but it was too heavy, too thick.

I turned, staring out the balcony window, but it was too high for me to jump.

He locked me in here.

My breaths came out ragged, my lungs tightening. I grabbed onto my chest as the panic started to form.

How could he lock me in?

Didn't he know?

God, didn't he know?

My body was drenched in sweat as I slid to the floor, trembling uncontrollably. I was having a panic attack, one I hadn't felt in years. I screamed. I screamed as my chest constricted, as my heart seemed to leap into my throat. I screamed knowing no one would hear me. And just as I thought I couldn't take it anymore, darkness and emptiness surrounded me.

Nine years ago...

"Where are you off too?"

My father's voice echoed in the empty hallway. He always seemed to appear out of nowhere. I didn't know him all that well, so I was still uncomfortable being near him. I had been brought up by my grandmother, and although I'd heard of him, I never met him until the funeral.

"And what are you wearing?"

I looked down at my white button-down shirt and blue and gray plaid skirt. "M-my school uniform?"

"You look like one of the whores in those titty bars."

I gasped, shocked that he'd talk to me in that way. My grandmother had brought me up to be a good girl, she'd even paid for me to go to private Catholic school because she always said she wanted the best education for me. My father was the complete opposite. He was a mangy creature from another planet.

From the moment I stepped into the Death Row Shooters clubhouse I knew this wasn't a place I wanted to be. But I had no choice. When grandma collapsed a few months ago I thought I could handle things myself, and I did for a while, until the money dwindled, and the hospital bills piled up. When she passed there was nothing else to do but to call a man I never knew.

She'd given me his name and number on her death bed. She'd told me he was the one to call if anything happened, he owed her that and so much more. So here I was, in his territory, and I hated every second of it.

"Come here," he grumbled, and I hesitated for a moment before approaching him.

I bit my cheek and clenched my fists as he ran his hands down my arms and twirled me around, playing with the hem of my skirt. "You have a tight little ass and great tits, maybe I'll put you to work at the bar."

I moved away from his hand that was running up my thigh. I hated the way he touched me, like he had a right over me, or like I was his property. I hated him.

"What? You don't like my hands on you, little girl. You better get used to men like me touching on you. The boys here don't play around. A sweet little pussy like yours could sell real good."

I clutched my skirt and took a step back. He gripped my wrist and I pulled back trying to get away. "Where the fuck do you think you're going?"

"I'm just going to school."

"You don't need to go to school. I'll show you how to make good money."

"No! Please," I sobbed as he dragged me toward him.

"You talkin' back to me, girl?"

I shook my head, afraid to say anything that would aggravate him. "I can see it in those damn eyes. You lookin' down on me. You remember one thing," his grip on my chin was brutal. "I'm still your fucking father!"

Tears fell down my face as he dragged me towards him. "Please. Please, I just want to go to school."

I looked back at my bookbag lying on the hallway floor, the door was there. It was right there. I pulled on his arm, but he gripped me tighter making me yelp out in pain.

"You need to learn discipline! I'll teach you what obedience means when you're under my roof."

"Please, Mario, please."

He turned, fury in his eyes. Snarling he leaned over me and I cowered. "I fucking gave you life, you call me Father, Dad, Sir, but you will not disrespect me!"

I flinched as he raised his hand, clenching it into a fist, before he lowered it and continued to drag me towards the back of the bar. He opened a door at the very back and threw me inside.

"Maybe this will teach you not to disrespect the President of the Death Row Shooters!"

He slammed the door shut and locked the door.

"No! Mari-Dad! Dad, please!"

It didn't matter what I said, he didn't come back. I searched the walls for a light switch, but there was none. It was pitch black and it smelled like mildew. In the silence I heard scuffling and then the squeal of a rat and I screamed. I was so damn scared I couldn't breathe. I'd never been mistreated in my life, always loved by my grandmother, respected by my teachers. I didn't understand why he would do this to me. I kicked at the door, I banged on it, and I yelled until I collapsed on the floor. I was tired, broken, my throat dry, my voice gone.

I fell asleep and was woken up by the sound of music, the base pounding through the door. It took me a moment to remember where I was, and then I felt something on my thigh. I screamed as I brushed it away and grabbing onto the doorknob, I staggered back up. I kicked at the door and yelled, but it was of no use. With the music swallowing my screams, no one could hear me.

The only stream of light came from beneath the door and once again I tried getting around the room, but I kept bumping into things, and still I couldn't find a switch. Feeling worn out I went back to the door, trying to scream for help but my voice was gone. In its place came silent cries as I slid back down to the floor. I curled myself against the door and cried until I couldn't anymore.

Slowly wariness engulfed me, and I lay my head down where the light streamed in and let darkness come. Voices stirred me awake and I had no idea what time it was. But the voices came closer, they became clearer, until they were right on the other side of the door. I pressed my ear to the door to listen.

"Yeah well, I don't know if I can trust any of these fuckers in here."

"Have you seen his daughter? How is that little girl associated with that beast?"

"She must have taken after her mother. Poor thing, I heard she's shaken up bad."

Who was that?

"I don't think she's gonna survive this place."

That voice was so familiar. What was his name?

"I know you like her man, but just be careful, you don't fuck around with the Prez's daughter."

"She's fifteen!"

The other man chuckled, and I remembered who he was. His name was Ryan Turner. I'd met him a few days ago when I was introduced to all the members. I remember I liked his eyes. He had nice eyes, and they didn't look at me like a piece of meat. He always treated me kindly. He was a good man. I had to believe that. I banged and kicked at the door. I had no energy or no voice, but I had to get out. I needed help. I needed his help.

"Shhh, you hear that?" The deeper voice got closer.

"What the hell is that?"

I banged harder at the door, shaking the door knob. "What the fuck is that?"

His voice was right there, in my ear, and I shook the

door knob again hoping and praying that they'd open the door.

"Is there someone in there?" His voice was at the crack of the door and I whispered his name. "There's someone in there, Ash."

"Stand back," the deeper voice spoke, but as he tried to yank the door open, it wouldn't budge.

I looked down at the doorknob and continued to pound on the door, faster this time. Knocking on it.

"Fuck!" I heard banging and the doorknob rattled until it dropped heavily onto the floor by my feet. The door swung open and I fell out, right into his arms.

"Oh shit," he uttered, holding me tight. "What are you doing here, pretty girl?"

My eyes met his, his voice gentle. I tried talking, but I could barely whisper. He got down to his knees, cradling me. "Get her some water!" He yelled out at the other man who stood near us. I barely glanced at him while I looked at my savior.

"Hey, Firefly," he whispered, pressing a gentle hand to my cheek. He reached up and reached for the glass, pressing it to my lips.

"How long has she been in there?" The man, Ash was his name, crouched down next to us.

"I don't know but maybe we should take her to see a doctor. She looks bad."

I gulped down the water and he held it away. "Slow down, Angel. Not too fast." Pressing it to my lips again he let me drink, and I couldn't help but stare into his eyes. He felt so safe, so warm.

"Who locked you up in there, Cecilia?"

I turned to look at Ash. "Mario," I croaked, coughing slightly.

"Motherfucker," Ryan whispered angrily.

He lifted me into his arms and started walking out the door. I was glad for that because there was no way I was going to be able to walk. I gripped onto his leather collar, afraid I was going to faint.

He sat me down in the back seat of the truck and shut the door. Instantly I started to feel constricted again, but then the doors opened, Ash slid into the front seat of the truck and Ryan slid in next to me, dragging me by his side.

He slid his hand along my forehead and I calmed at his touch. "Sleep firefly. I got you. Sleep."

Closing my eyes, I let sleep take me over. When I woke up, I was in the hospital, diagnosed with dehydration and malnutrition. I was put on an IV and told that I needed to stay overnight. I lay in the dark, staring at the ceiling. I was left alone in the room while Ryan and Ash went to go get some food. I smiled when I thought of Ryan. He didn't want to leave my side, but I told him he had to go eat. Ash dragged him out winking at me as he shut the door.

Tears fell down my cheeks as I remembered the darkness of that old storage closet. There were rats in that space and the doctors checked me for any bites or scratch marks. I did have a few on my thighs and they had to test me for rabies. This is where I had fallen, and there didn't seem to be much escape.

Ryan walked in and he furrowed his brow as he was followed by two police officers. He stepped to my side and slid his hand into mine. "The police want to talk to you, Cecilia."

I looked up at him and he just squeezed my hand. "Just tell them the truth," he whispered.

But what was the truth? That my father had locked me in an old abandoned storage closet and forgotten about me. I stared up at Ryan and he nodded while the officer asked his questions.

"Can you tell us what happened to you, Miss Cepeda?"

My grandmother always taught me that family comes first. That we needed to protect each other. I was at a crossroads and I chose the path I shouldn't have.

"I locked myself into a closet and Ryan found me."

Both the officer and Ryan looked down on me and Ryan leaned in. "Are you sure, Firefly?"

I nodded. "Yes, I was looking for something and forgot that the door locked on its own. I was in there for at least twenty-four hours."

I avoided Ryan's eyes because I knew what they were saying. *Coward.*

The officer took the rest of the statement and left. Ryan paced back in forth in front of my bed, he'd look at me like he was about to say something, and then he'd continue to pace. He finally stopped and propped his fists on the foot of the bed.

"Why?"

I bit my trembling lip, tears forming in my eyes. "He's all I have left, Ryan."

He shook his head. "He treats you like shit!"

"But he's all I have left," I sobbed, and he came over to me, hugging me and holding me tight.

"I can be someone for you, Firefly. You can lean on me whenever you need to."

His sincerity warmed my heart and I clung to that feeling, something I hadn't felt since my grandmother died. This was only the beginning of my turmoil with my father, if I wouldn't have been so naïve, but I was a little girl who needed love and thought this was the only way to go.

10

RYAN

Present day...

Digger, my main Enforcer, sat in an old brown leather chair against the far back wall. Christopher *Digger* Schield, had been voted in a few years back when we were just starting out. An ex-marine, brutal as fuck, and we found out quick that he was a good man to have at your back when shit went down. Especially when he saved my life on our first ride. He was savvy in all types of weapons combat and was in charge of training new prospects and the rest of the Patches who wanted to learn. Every once in a while, he was useful in doing other shit around this place. At this particular moment, he was sitting there, playing with a razor blade, removing black paint from beneath his fingertips. He'd been painting the sign outside for The Den earlier this morning.

"Hey man, I told you to paint the sign, not to paint yourself."

"You have no idea what the fuck happened to me."

I shook my head and smirked. "Looks like you got the bucket of paint dumped all over you."

He narrowed his eyes on me and I chuckled as Ash walked in slapping me on the back and taking a seat beside Digger. "What the fuck happened to you?"

"Fell on his ass outside," Poet muttered as he sauntered in with Crow. Max Sinclair, better known as Crow, was an edgy motherfucker. He'd also been part of the Devil's Syndicate a few years back. According to him, they'd done him wrong, and he wanted out. So when he knocked on the Death Row Shooters door we had to make sure he wouldn't turn his back on us like he did the Syndicate. A couple years back we had some issues with Tuco Moreno, and he took a shot for me. Two days later he was voted in as our new Tail Gunner.

In the opposite end of the room stood the Vindicator. Jayce Williams, the Death Row Shooters Chaplain was an emotionless, hard headed son of a bitch, but he was one of my most trusted members and friends. Although we argued all the time, he always gave sage advice and I wouldn't be here if it wasn't for him, Poe & Ash. He was the old Chaplain, friend to Nate, he'd left when Nate died. In order to make the Death Row Shooters what they were, I needed him by my side, and he was happy to return the help.

"What did you find out?"

Ash leaned forward and arched a brow. "You're not gonna like what I have to say."

"Just fuckin' say it."

"There's some serious shit going down on the docks. Large fucking shipments coming in from China. I don't think word has gotten around as to who owns those docks."

"Sex trafficking?" I asked, wary of the answer.

Poe shook his head. "Not women, but they're trafficking some big money items. Stolen goods."

"Does Wolf know about this?"

"Not unless Riggs was around and I haven't seen him for a few days."

"Good. I don't want the Hellbound Lovers knowing our shit. I've already paid my debt, I don't want them prying in Death Row Shooters business."

"If this continues it will be hard to keep anything from them, but I'll try to do as you say."

I nodded. "What else?"

"We tracked one of the men down. Guess where he went?"

I thought for a minute and smiled. "Ravenous?"

Ash shook his head. "Closer."

I looked from Ash to Poe and then slapped my knee. "Unbelievable! My Den."

They both nodded. Poe stepped further into the room. "I sent one of the girls to spy on him."

"Who?"

"You ain't gonna like what I'm about to say, Prez."

"Who?"

"Brandy."

I narrowed my eyes on him and heard Jayce shift behind me. "Are you kidding me? Do you not know who that girl is?"

Poe nodded. "I know, but they took a liking to her. She was the only one who could get in their heads."

"I'll fucking kill you, man."

I slammed the back of my hand against Jayce's chest, stopping him from pummeling down on Poe. He wasn't gonna win and we both knew it. He had a soft spot for the girl, and I couldn't blame him. Sweet tight ass, young, and she was dancing on our stages, but she had a dark past. Her husband was an ex-cop, a crooked son of a bitch, and when she came to the Chaplain he couldn't refuse her a job. She was under his protection, the fact that Poe had used her was not in his favor.

"She's fine, Brother. You've got a good one there. She knows how to work it hard and she got what we needed."

"Using pussy for intel. Fucked up, Brother."

Poe shrugged. "Who's gonna say no to nice young pussy."

"Motherfucker!" Jayce lunged over me and grabbed at him, but Poe simply raised his hands and took a step back.

"Sorry, Brother. I don't know what she did, but she got us some serious info. According to her, the guy worked as a middle-man, taking in shipments of art. Statues, paintings, sculptures, all cloaked so that no one would be the wiser."

I nodded and urged him to continue. "Apparently they are here to meet their dealer."

"Dealer?"

Ash spoke up next. "So, I did some research." He stood and handed me a card, the name Priscilla Chantal was scrawled along the back of the card, along the front was the name KAI Art Galleria in copper letters, a number printed along the bottom.

"Looks like Miss Chantal runs a gallery in Beverly Hills. Does well for herself and as far as I can tell is the sole owner."

"Could be a front," I stated.

Ash shrugged. "Brandy's a good girl. She must have sucked some decent cock for the next bit of information we got."

I could sense Jayce tensing next to me and I narrowed my eyes on Ash. "Respect, Ash."

He gave Jayce an arrogant smirk and continued. "Looks like the China man comes in, gets the goods from the girl, and transports them back to Hong Kong."

"So he's a babysitter**?"**

"More or less. In exchange, he gets a hefty sum of money. Money he was more than willing to invest into Brandy."

"I'm gonna kill you," Jayce muttered under his breath and I knew the boys were fucking with him. He was always down their throats and they seemed to be wanting some payback. Problem was, it was on my time, and their games were short lived.

"Stop fuckin' around. Brandy was not the woman to choose for this shit. What if she would have gotten hurt? What if she would have gotten caught?"

Poe sighed. "Girl's smart, gave him a lap dance, humped his cock a bit, gave him a kiss and left. Probably creamed his pants." He looked up at Jayce. "No need to worry, Brother, I had my eyes on her the whole time. Fucker came back though, the following night. Wanted a little more than a lap dance and I had Crow there, kick him the fuck out."

"So, he's a fence, a middle man. She's the seller," I lifted the card and took a long look at it. "Who is the buyer?"

Poe shrugged. "We don't know. All we know is that the buyer comes from Hong Kong."

"So how much money are we talking about?"

"As far as I can tell," Ash rubbed his thick beard, "a good half a mil to a mil for shipment alone. Looks like the toughest part for the dealer is finding a dock."

"Fuck me," I sat up, all ears now. "Make sure the Hell-bound Lovers don't get a wind of this shit."

Poe nodded. "I'll let Riggs know we're moving coffee

grounds or something. That way we can keep them off our radar."

"Alright then." I twirled the card around, sweeping my thumb across the name. "I think we need to pay a visit to Miss Chantal."

11

RYAN

"Cecilia?" I knocked on the door before sliding it open. It was oddly dark in the bedroom making it hard to see anything.

"Cecilia?" I pushed the door wide open. The stream of light coming in from the hallway fell on her body, strewn on the ground.

"Cecilia!" I ran over to her, coming down on my knees as I lifted her into my arms. "Baby? Baby talk to me." I brushed her hair away from her face. She was drenched in cold sweat and was shaking.

"Cecilia, for fuck's sake!"

Her eyes fluttered open and shut, her head moving from side to side. She uttered something beneath her breath that I couldn't make out. I leaned in closer while she repeated it nonstop.

"You left me. You left me."

"Nooo baby, no. I didn't leave you. I'm right here. I'm right here." I rocked her in my arms, the hurt that was between us, threatening to destroy us both.

"You left me," she whispered in my ear and I held her so tight.

"I will never leave you, Firefly. I will never leave you.

"You forgot me." Her voice broke and it tore at my heart.

Memories of her locked in that damn closet came to me and I cursed myself for forgetting. I cursed myself for being so goddamn stupid. "It's alright baby, I'm right here. I'm so sorry. I'm so fucking sorry."

I stayed with her all night, soothing her until she stopped shaking. Staring up at the ceiling while I remembered the fear on her young face when we found her locked up that day. I felt helpless as she fell into my arms. I think I fell in love with her in those moments, I just didn't know what the feeling was. Love was such a farfetched thought back then. But now, now I knew. I knew what this tightening in my chest, this lightheadedness that overcame me when I had her in my arms, what this desperation meant. She could deny it all she wanted to, but I knew. I knew she loved me just as much or more.

I left early the next morning after I made sure she was alright. When Ash walked into the room he nearly murdered me when I told him I'd locked her in. That memory still looming over her, still harming her.

Fuck.

I was a fucking shit bag to her. My selfish ways only hurt her. But I was scared. I was fucking frightened of losing her. The President of the Death Row Shooters had a fear. A fear that he held secret. A fear that would get us both killed if I wasn't careful.

We rode out to the Galleria with Ash. If this Priscilla Chantal woman was a front, I didn't want to scare her with a bunch of bikers approaching. Instead, we decided to take the truck, or what we liked to call the Cage. I wore my business suit and Ash, well Ash wore his cuts but at least his dark washed jeans looked new. He wore a white tee beneath his leather vest, tattoos lined his muscled arms hiding his scars, and he had a deadpanned look in his eye as we entered the Galleria.

"You need to relax, Ash. We're here to buy art not shoot up the place."

"You never know when you have to watch your back, Prez."

He was right about that. These pristine white walls would drip with fresh red blood quite nicely. Our boots clicked on the shined hardwood floor, bright colored art aligned each sectional, and above us sculptured glass blown chandeliers hung at different angles.

"Looks like an art gallery to me," I looked over at Ash and he just shrugged, his attention on a sculpture in the corner with a naked couple holding each other. I smirked as his hand grazed her breasts.

"Perv," I muttered under my breath and proceeded to make my way towards the small reception area.

The place was empty, there wasn't a soul in sight. Clearing my throat, I yelled out. "Hello? Anyone here?"

My voice echoed and suddenly the sound of heels came from beyond the sectioned walls. Ash approached my right side as we waited. The sound getting closer until a woman peeked her head around the corner. When she fully appeared, Ash tensed beside me, and I had to admit, she was a sight. Tall, dark hair that flowed in soft waves down her back, big bright coffee colored eyes and the prettiest face. Not as pretty as my Cecilia, but hot damn this one was gorgeous.

Her hunter green dress clung to ever fucking curve, the voluminous tits, the wide hips, the rounded perfect ass. We both stood there appreciating the fucking art.

"Can I help you, gentlemen?"

Her accent was sexy as fuck and Ash shifted next to me. The motherfucker probably had a wicked hard on, and the way she was eyeing him, I'm pretty sure he'd have her in his bed calling him Daddy before the night was over.

I slid her card on the receptionist's high counter and I stared at her. "I'm here to talk business with the owner of this gallery."

She took the card and smiled. I knew this card meant something because it was completely different to the white card sitting on the receptionist's counter. "I'm the owner."

I arched my brow in surprise and looked over at Ash who couldn't keep his eyes off her ass. "Which means you are Miss Chantal."

"That is correct," she turned her head slightly, looking over at Ash who was now circling her like a fucking predator.

"Ash!" I called out and he instantly straightened up and walked over to me, a glint in his eye. "Ash here and myself have noticed some movements on my docks. Word is Kai Galleria has a bit of business going on there. I don't know if you were aware, but those docks are private property. My property."

I could sense in her eyes that she was fully aware, but she was a great actress. "No, I'm sorry. I have no idea what you are talking about."

She turned to leave, but Ash was right behind her. She gasped as he wrapped his hand around her waist and slowly turned her back around to face me. I let him have his fun. I'm pretty sure his dick was jumping in excitement to be pressed against her ass as he held her there for me to speak with.

"I could easily call the feds on you, but I won't. Not unless you decide to give me wrong information. I don't take lightly to lies."

She gave out a broken gasp as Ash gave his hand a little jerk, squeezing her tighter. "I suggest you tell the man the truth, honey."

"I believe we can help each other out here, Miss Chantal. What kind of business are you running on my docks?"

"None of your business."

"Eh, eh," Ash whispered in her ear and the woman was literally putty in his hands. "Be nice or I'll have to punish you later."

Her eyes went wide, and she bit her lip, shifting slightly against him. His grunt told me she was also playing his game.

"It's my business when you're on my private property. So I suggest we work together instead of against each other."

"What do you propose?"

"I heard there's shipments being made with a certain group of men that are being paid a hefty sum. My understanding is you need to pay for the docks and the transportation. Unfortunately, I haven't seen a cent of those payments."

"It is hard to find good men these days. Besides, I have nothing to do with how they store or transport the items, as long as they get to the right owners on time."

"What's in the crates?"

"Art. Hot items. Items that if I do not get to my bosses in Hong Kong they will be very upset."

"What do these middlemen mean to you?"

"Nothing. They come from Hong Kong. From the buyer."

"And who are your bosses?"

"I cannot tell you that. The walls have ears and eyes," she looked up and sure enough, right above us was a camera.

I nodded. "Tell your boss that I am willing to give you full access to my docks, without calling the Feds, as long as my men and I can transport the goods."

Her eyes shone, and her eyebrows furrowed. "Why?"

"Because, Miss Chantal. I am a businessman. Ask around. I'm pretty sure your bosses know me. Ryan Simon is my name, but you can call me the Reaper." I slid her one of my cards with the Death Row Shooters logo on the front. "We can negotiate a price and in return we'll offer you protection. It's up to you Miss Chantal, how you want to proceed. But I can assure you, you either work with us, or those docks are off limits. I'll be waiting for your call."

"You are not giving me much of a choice, Mr. Simon."

"That's not the way we negotiate. You've been using my docks, there are no choices in this deal. The only one you have is call me or wait for the feds to coming knocking at your door."

"We don't like to be threatened."

"Oh that's not a threat, honey. You wanted a choice, I gave you one."

Winking, I turned and walked away. I could hear her moan as I stepped out the doors, God knows what Ash was doing to the poor woman. No woman could resist Ash Warden. I leaned back on the Cage until Ash came out with a big grin on his face.

"You got your kicks off?"

"Let's just say she'll definitely be calling you."

I smirked and slid into the passenger seat. As we took off, a text rang through.

You can meet me at the docks tomorrow before sunrise. We'll negotiate then.

"Looks like she took the bait."

Ash didn't say a word, but by the way his grip tightened on the steering wheel, I had a feeling he had a lot to do in persuading the beauty.

12

CECILIA

THE MUSIC and energy from two floors below caught my attention. Ryan had rebuilt on the land that used to be the clubhouse. The first floor held the club, the bar, and private rooms along the inside of the floor, hidden from sight. Ryan's office was on the second floor looking over his club and there were six apartments that spanned out either sides of the office. The executive members lived on the second floor. The third floor was off limits to everyone but me and Ryan. It was his private home and he owned the entire floor. From the outside it looked like any apartment complex, but inside it was huge. An entire mansion all to himself.

A balcony ran along the outside of the apartments looking down onto the dance floor. Since I'd been here, I'd never actually gone into the club, but tonight the music captured me. I wanted to see something other than the dim light in my bedroom, and after a nice long shower I felt renewed, wanting to go out.

When I came out into the hallway, the music pumping through the floorboards and the flashing lights beckoned me. The strobe lights flashed across the building, highlighting the dancefloor. I saw the girls on the stages, twirling on the poles. Couples danced on the floor while men in suits lounged around talking business or throwing their money away at the next girl that stepped onto the platform. There was a girl on the side of the platform, she had short red hair and a body to kill for. She swayed in the cage, rocking her hips side to side while Jayce, the one they called the Vindicator, stood right beneath it. The look in his eye, a challenge to any man who dared approach her. I found the sight intriguing.

"What are you doing out here?"

I startled at the sound of his voice and turned to find his eyes on my body. I'd stepped out in just a pale pink slip I'd found in one of the drawers. Ryan had thought of everything, even going to the extreme of buying me clothes and every pair of shoes you could imagine. A whole walk in closet just for me. Any woman would want that, any woman except me. I lived a simple life, and if he thought I cared about any of this, he was sorely mistaken.

"You're not supposed to be here."

"I came home early," his rumble had me biting my lip.

I hadn't expected Ryan for another day or so. But here he was, half hidden in shadows, his dark eyes locked on me, and he looked so damn sexy in his rolled-up sleeves that exposed his muscled forearms, flexing as he shoved his golden waves back. He was wearing all black with shiny black boots. Fuck, the man was lickable even with his clothes on.

"I asked you a question."

"I-I was just curious."

He took the few steps towards me and pulled me away

from the balcony. In his haste, he shoved me roughly up against the wall, his arms caging me in. He looked different tonight, he had a hungry gleam in his eye I hadn't seen before.

"Curious about what, baby?"

A lock of his golden hair fell over his eye and caressed my cheek. Hanging his head I could feel his breath along my neck. I went weak for him and clung to the wall praying he wouldn't notice.

"I just wanted to take a look. See what happens in the club."

"And what did you see?"

"Just the girls dancing."

"Do you dance, Firefly?" His growl made me so damn hot. I was fighting it, but he had this absolute control over me.

"Occasionally," I sighed while running my hands along his broad chest.

"Hmmm...I can sense how wet you are, baby." His nose brushed along the curve of my neck and he inhaled me.

"Your pussy smells so fucking good."

"Stop," I barely whispered, my word holding no strength in it whatsoever. It was more a hidden plea for him to continue.

My breath caught as his hand ran up my bare thigh, goosebumps resonating through my body. I'd only just stepped out for a second, not ever expecting to come across anyone, least of all him. He was supposed to be away, out doing a job. I had no idea he'd be back so soon.

"What are you doing?" I breathed, shaking beneath his touch.

"I can't stay away from you," his husky confession made me bite back a moan.

"Ryan, please."

"Fuck, I love the sound of you begging." I inhaled sharply as his fingers traced the seam of my panties. His electrifying blue eyes met mine, his face hidden in shadows. My lips parted as his fingers dove beneath the silk fabric, tracing the smoothness of my swollen core.

"Fuck," he breathed, as he fell to his knees before me. There was a devilish look in his eyes as he slid his hands up my thighs, massaging the thick flesh and urging my legs apart. His hands groped my hips and cupped my ass before gripping the waistband of my panties. He teased me, snapping the waistband against my skin and smiling as I rotated my hips for him. He bit at the soft flesh at my tummy before sliding the soft material slowly down my legs. My hands clenched on either side of me, a moment of confusion clashing with reality as my panties slipped to the floor.

"Ryan," The sound of uncertainty echoed in the empty hallway and I reached down, placing my hands over his, but there was no slowing this man down.

"Yes, Cecilia," the heavy rumble of his voice made me tremble. That promise of pleasure lingering in the air around us. My hands covering his as they slid up my bare legs, lifting my slip until his groan informed me that he'd exposed my core.

I leaned my head back, a prayer leaving my lips at the feel of his hot breath that ran along my most private of body parts, making me wet with need. "Ryan, what are you doing to me?"

He gripped my thighs, his breath coming out in uneven bursts. "Driving you crazy."

I cried out as his tongue dragged along my slit, his rumble of satisfaction vibrating against my clit just before his tongue curled and sucked me in. My body reacted instantly to him, my legs shaking uncontrollably as he opened me wide, propping me up and hooking me onto his broad shoulders, giving him full access to my pussy while his tongue sank into me. I gripped the wall to steady myself, but my hips danced along his beard on their own accord. There was no stopping this pleasure. Even if I wanted to, I couldn't. He felt too good, too right, his tongue extending and flattening, gathering up all my juices before he sucked on my most tender of areas. I gripped his hair and yelled out his name, not caring if anyone heard. My juices flowing as his mouth consumed my pussy.

His fingers dug into the flesh of my ass as he lapped hungrily at my core, his breath swirling along my clit, the coarseness of his beard rubbing along my sensitive skin. I shook in his arms, my hands clawing at the wall, unable to utter a sound as he took what he wanted from me.

"You are the sweetest of sins, Firefly. So fucking addictive." The sound of him sucking on me had my hips rotating against him. Fucking his tongue just like he wanted me to.

"I want you cumming on my tongue every night, Cecilia."

"Ryan!" I cried his name out in a needy shout as his teeth scraped my clit, dragging along the tight bud. My hips went wild, undulating against his handsome face while my fingers dug into his thick locks of golden hair.

His tongue played along my lips, sucking and nipping, groaning as he ate me up. Lips pressed to my swollen core as his tongue dug into my hot hole, making me whimper as he curled it up, knowing just what to do to elicit the sluttiest of moans from me. I panted as his tongue dug into me, his lips suctioning, his fingers spreading me.

He focused on my clit, flicking it and biting it until I was a quivering mess in his hands. And right when I didn't think I could handle anymore, his thick fingers sunk into me, penetrating me slowly as his lips wrapped around that sensitive button. I squealed and convulsed as his fingers fucked me up against that wall. The combination of his hot mouth and those two digits curling up inside me was my undoing. My body tensed, my fingers gripped his hair, and I came for him. My juices spilling on his tongue, and the image of me coating his face with my cream sent me soaring.

It was so dirty, so wrong.

I took gulps of air and stared out at the silhouette of colorful lights that reflected from below. Slowly, he let my slip fall back into place and I looked down just as he tucked away my panties into his back pocket. He stood before me, his lips only a fraction of an inch from mine.

Gripping my chin, he brought his lips to mine and growled. "Suck me in baby girl. Taste yourself on my tongue." I gasped as he slipped his tongue against mine, the taste of my juices lingering as our tongues dueled in an erotic dance. No one kissed like Ryan did. In his kiss I could feel the want, the hunger he held for me, and I didn't hold back how much I wanted him in return. I molded my body to his, loving the feel of his hardness pressed against me. I needed more from him, so much more, but instead he broke the kiss and stepped away from me.

"Go to your room, Cecilia. I don't want anyone seeing what's mine."

With those words spoken, he left me there. Needing him even more than before. This man was going to drive me insane. He was beyond any fantasy, he was my reality. He was passionate and unselfish, and he wanted *me*. With weak legs I stumbled back into the apartment and shut the door. My head thumped back against it and I closed my eyes. I pictured his penetrating blue eyes, those tattoos that moved along his muscled torso, the way his beard felt between my thighs. My fingers played along the seam of my slip, sliding to where his mouth had been only seconds before. A deep moan emanated from me while I stood in the empty apartment and stroked myself, imaging him between my legs once again.

13
RYAN

IT WAS three in the morning and I couldn't fucking sleep. Tossing and turning, the taste of her cunny still on my lips. She'd become mine without knowing it, just hours before and my cock was unsatisfied, hard and throbbing for her. I already blew a load to her once in the shower, picturing her on her knees before me. Again, while I was having a drink in the living room. I leaned my head back on the couch imagining her watching me stroke my cock for her. I pictured her needy and aching as she slid that pussy down my thickness, her tits swaying erotically in front of my eyes as she screamed out my name. Grunting I sprayed my thighs and chest in my white seed. Seed that belonged deep inside of her.

Getting up, I wandered to the bathroom, taking my cock out I let the stream go, sighing at the temporary relief. If I didn't get some sleep I wouldn't be able to do what I needed to do tomorrow. The meeting was to be at the docks early in the morning, meaning in three hours. I was never going to make it.

I passed by Cecilia's bedroom door and then stopped,

walking back to it. I reached for the door knob, my hand itching to turn it. I paused for a second and waited. Silence. Absolute silence.

Just do it. Fucking do it. Who the fuck cares about the consequences. She belongs to you.

I slipped through the door, wandering barefoot into her room. She'd left the bathroom light on, the door propped open to let some light in. She was curled on her side, right at the edge of the bed, even though it was a massive king-sized mattress. Pulling my briefs off, I crawled onto the bed, sliding myself behind her. I groaned into her hair at the feel of her bare ass nuzzling my cock. My hands came around her waist and my dick responded when I realized she was naked in bed.

"Fuck, baby girl. Do you want to destroy me?" She shifted in her sleep as I cupped her large swollen globes. Flicking her dark nipples, she gasped.

"Ryan?" She struggled against my hips, but I held her still.

"It's me, baby. Just me." I pet and cooed at her until she finally relaxed in my arms.

She was so soft, felt so right in my arms. I couldn't stop touching her, stroking her leg and letting my hand wander around her hips. I could feel her tense slightly just as goose-bumps formed on her flesh. I let my fingertips glide along her inner thigh, but when I went to spread her legs apart, she squeezed them tightly together. I heard the hitch in her breath-felt the tension in her back.

"Let me in, my sweet girl. I won't hurt you." Slowly I slid my hand between her legs and after a moment of hesitation, she parted her thighs allowing me to hook her leg up and over my hip. I spread her wide as my fingernails dragged along her plump flesh. My rough palms stroking up and down her body, making her whimper from my heated touch.

"Ryan," she whispered huskily as I nuzzled her slender neck.

"Ryan, please," the plea getting caught in her throat as my fingers delved into her sweet pussy.

"Just let me touch you, Cecilia. Let me feel you, just once. I missed you so damn much," without waiting for a reply my fingers slid through her wet slit. I growled in satisfaction as her body responded, arching back and whimpering.

"So soft," I murmured and nipped at her ear. She grunted and squirmed against me, blood filling the head of my cock and making it swell. She cried out when I flicked her already hardened clit and nearly leapt off the bed when I dipped one thick finger inside her honey hole.

"So wet for me, so perfect," I purred all the right things into her ear, the dirty words exciting her, drenching my hand in her juices as her body instinctively primed her for more.

"I want my tongue on your pussy again. I want to taste you, Cecilia."

I slid down the bed, leaving her side briefly and I loved how the lack of having me made her whimper needily. Sliding between her legs, I blew a hot breath against her glistening pussy lips, her honey already coating them. Gripping the sheets, she tensed, knowing what was going to happen next.

I stroked her gently, outlining her lips and spreading her cream all over them, teasing her. "Look at me, little girl. Watch as your savior tastes you for the second time."

She bit her lip as she finally brought herself to look at

me. Grinning, I winked at her, just as I stuck out my thick tongue, dragging it across her core.

"Oh!" her cry of pleasure made me smile against her pussy, her hips lifted and my cock pulsed against the mattress. My hips rocked steadily, a desperate need to be inside her. I was like a hungry beast devouring her slickened horny flesh. I slurped on her pussy as if it were a sweet peach I couldn't get enough of. Lapping at her delicate folds, loving how her head flew black when I rimmed her tiny entrance. Her hips raised again and grabbing her ass I held her there, perched in the air as my lips closed around that excited little bud, flicking it until she was panting and squealing my name.

"Fuck!" I watched as she gripped the sheets and bowed back, her legs spreading wider as sweet heat ran through her body. My tongue incessantly drawing out her need as she lay completely at my mercy.

Her fingers reached down and stroked my head, grabbing a handful of my hair. Holding me captive between the crevice of her thighs, she started to rub her sweet pussy on my face. Up and down as my tongue went wild on her, her ragged breaths made her tits bounce lightly on her curvy frame and she screamed when I began to suck on her clit. Her legs shook, and the sweetest orgasm travelled slowly through her body until she finally exploded on my tongue, my name rolling sexily off her lips.

I hummed as I lapped at her soothingly, my grin never fading. "You cum so well, my sweet girl."

"Ryan," her voice trembling as I softly licked at her, gathering her creaminess on my tongue.

"I can't get enough of your taste, Cecilia. So sweet, like the most addictive fruit. Have you ever let anyone else touch what's mine, Firefly? Has anyone else ever touched you like this?"

She shut her eyes and I waited, I didn't realize how much I needed that answer. I didn't want to hear that another man had touched her. I was her one and only.

She looked at me, uncertainty in her gaze as she confessed. "There have been several others. Don't think for a second that you're the only one because you're not. Now if you're done you can get out."

She went to turn on her side and I growled, crawling over her body and holding her in place. Her eyes widened when she realized I was right above her, a whimper of fear escaping. I knew my eyes must have frightened her because she raised her hands and pressed them against my chest, warding me off. I felt like the hungry wolf and she was my frail prey.

"Not the only one? Don't lie to me now."

"Yes," her voice continued to shake as I rubbed my hard length along her core. Her legs spread wide for me, completely exposed, unknowingly telling me to take her and do what I wanted to her.

"Liar," my fingertips grazed her lips and I leaned down and captured them in a slow, sultry kiss. I humped at her, wild in my need for her. She couldn't help but rub herself against me, my hard length sliding up through her warm slit. She cried out when my velvety cock stroked her swollen clit, teasing her.

I grunted, my breath hitching at the heated sensation. I moved my hips in waves as I continued to hump at her. "I want you so badly, baby. But don't be scared. I won't be taking you tonight, Cecilia. Not until you beg me." She avoided my eyes and I tugged her chin forward. "And you will beg me. You will eventually be mine, even though you like to fight me."

I sat up on my knees and lifted her into my arms, she wanted to play games, fine. She wouldn't last long. Sitting her on my lap I groaned, loving the wet heat of her slickened pussy consume my hardness. "Do it. Glide that sweet pussy on my cock. Feel it, Cecilia. Feel what I have kept from you for so long."

I closed my mouth around a dewy drop and sucked her flesh making her hips grind down on my dick. Her pussy lips parted as it slid along my girth while her tits glistened from my tongue. God, she was so perfect, so delicious. She felt like a dainty little doll perched upon my lap, being used at my will. I grabbed at her hips and helped her along, our bodies melting into one another.

"Ryan!" She cried out as the head of my cock bumped along her clit. Over and over, shocks of pleasure ran through me and I held onto her in my desperate need to cum. No one had ever had this impact on my body. She fucking belonged in my arms.

"More," her hot breath in my ear travelled to my enlarged groin making it leak for her. We both looked down and moaned as my cream made a mess along her swollen lips.

"When I take this sweet, tight pussy, you better believe you'll never leave my side again. You won't want another cock inside of you, not ever. Just mine."

"Ryan. Please."

"You're mine, my sweet girl. You always have been. Now cum for me. Let go and cum all over my cock."

We both moaned in ecstasy as my words drove us into a frenzy. Bodies sliding wetly together, wrapping around each other as we worked ourselves up to that release. When we came it was hot and dirty, and it made me want to sink deep inside of her and claim her. My cock throbbed between my legs as it pumped its hot cum against her inner thighs and bare core. Her hips still undulating, still sliding against me while she shook in my arms. She could deny anything she wanted, but she couldn't deny the fact that we were perfect for each other.

When we were through I lay her down and cuddled back up against her. My semi erect cock rested against the crevice of her ass, and when she pushed back on me, I chuckled into her neck.

"Don't play games now, Cecilia. I could take you right now if I wanted to. Don't push me."

She lay still in my arms then, knowing it wasn't the right time. Knowing this was enough for now. And as she drifted off into a deep sleep, I was also aware, that I'd been the only man in her life all this time. My sweet Firefly was a needy little thing. Needy for me, and for some reason that made my blood pump hard through my veins. This beautiful, delicate woman had a willingness to give herself to me that overwhelmed me. If only she'd let me, I'd make her the happiest fucking woman in the world.

14

RYAN

I HEADED out at four in the morning. I hated leaving her by herself, but I needed to get to the meeting point. I was pretty sure Ash and Poe were already there. I pulled up to the warehouse across from the docks. The buildings had been abandoned for quite some time and when we acquired the docks I made sure to acquire the properties surrounding it.

Entering the empty warehouse, I waited a moment. Hushed whispers and a moan caught my attention. Rolling my eyes I walked into the middle of the warehouse and searched the grounds. High windows let enough light seep through to see where the hell I was going.

Another moan and then the sound of Ash's rough voice made me roll my eyes. The next phrase had me gritting my teeth.

"This sweet pussy is mine for the taking."

"Ash!" I called out and almost immediately I heard scurrying. Within seconds Ash walked out from a back closet, zippering his pants up. He smirked as he walked over to me, a smug look in his eye.

"Can't you fucking keep your dick in your pants?"

He shrugged and looked over at the door where the pretty brunette emerged from. "Can you blame me?"

I shook my head and in truth I couldn't. Shit, no man could blame him. Fixing her bright yellow dress, she lifted her long thick locks to one side and strutted towards us.

"Fuck. Me." I heard him utter under his breath and I sighed.

"You don't shit where you eat," I uttered under my breath.

"I'm gonna marry that woman."

I raised a brow and greeted the woman in question. "Miss Chantal."

"Mr. Simon. Please," she gestured at the two chairs that had been set up in the middle of the room. "I took the liberty of securing the area. No one will be able to listen in on our conversation."

"Why so many secrets?"

"Have you ever worked with art before, Mr. Simon?"

"Never," I admitted.

"In the artist's mind they conjure an image, it is your interpretation of that image that matters the most. Why do you think all the secrecy?"

"Because you're playing games that you shouldn't."

"It's a cat and mouse game, Mr. Simon. A chase to see who can get away the fastest, who has the quickest transportation, the most creative way of hiding things."

"I see. And in this case?"

"In this case my bosses are aware of your reputation, Mr. Simon. They state you are to be trusted."

"To an extent, yes. But there are stipulations to that trust."

"Well trust should be earned, Mr. Simon."

"What are you saying? Speak clearly I don't like talking in circles."

"This will be your test run. The men we've been working with I'm afraid are not reputable. We are trying to keep this under wraps for your sake."

I narrowed my eyes on her and she shifted in her seat, rightly so. Her gazed flicked to Ash's before it steadied on me. "They have been stealing from me and my dealers for a long time. I have to admit that we are not happy with them and have been looking for an out of this contract. If you can prove yourself then we can work together."

"Who are these men you are seeming to want to protect us from?"

"Men that shouldn't be trifled with. But we hear you have a good reputation among the gangs of Los Angeles as well as several of those in the Asian community."

"I work my way around the circle. This is why I intend to earn your trust."

She nodded-her hands twisting on her lap-the only sign that she was nervous. "The first shipment will come in today. I like this set up you have here. If we are to work with you we would need a few guarantees as well as a signed contract.

I nodded in agreement. "My man, Poe, will get that to you. Our stipulations and demands and you can discuss the details with him."

"Perfect."

"Who are the buyers?"

"We have a large selection of buyers, all through the black market. Hong Kong is a big city, easy to get lost in. Shady business deals are made on the regular. The buyer requests the item, and we procure it. No questions asked. They get their item, we get our money."

"I see. So who exactly are we supposed to be handing this shipment to."

"There is a woman there, similar to me. Her name is Kai, she runs Kai Enterprises in the Tai Po district of Hong Kong. She is your liaison. Tell your man that if he finds her, he'll find the buyer."

"My man Poe has agreed to travel with the first shipment. He has a man there who can help him navigate through the cities."

"Very well. My best advice is that he keeps his head down and stays to himself. Foreigners attract attention. Attention we do not want. Half a million will be deposited into your account by morning, the other half will be deposited as soon as the shipment has been dispensed to the appropriate buyers."

"How do I know you guarantee my man's safety?"

"I don't guarantee anyone's safety, Mr. Simon. I pay you to guarantee the safety of my item. Trust me, you don't want to go against the people I work with. Nor do you want to be seen by those you are stealing from."

"Stealing?"

"I am breaking a contract for you to keep your mouth shut. You do the job right the contract is yours. You do it wrong and it's your head, including the pretty girl that lives with you. She will be used as collateral."

I clenched my fists and Ash shifted towards me. Not one word was spoken but I could sense the intensity in the glare he was giving her.

"You leave her alone."

"You asked for the job. This is how we work. You threatened me, Mr. Simon. That was your first mistake. Lose the shipment, and that will be a tragedy."

I clenched my jaw, keeping the vile retort from slipping

from my tongue. "You touch one hair on her head and I will have all of Los Angeles after you and the people you work with."

She nodded. "Fair enough. I only do the negotiations. You do what you will with the information I've given. But I urge you. Do not take my warnings lightly. The men who had this contract are dangerous. As soon as they find out that they will no longer be used they will go after you and yours. So, please, I beg you. Tell your man to be careful."

A few minutes later Ash and I walked out onto the docks. The wind swirled around us as we stood looking out onto the black water.

"Are you thinking what I'm thinking?"

I nodded. "What the fuck did we just get ourselves into?"

"We could back out?"

"I threatened them in order to take over. I won't back out of the deal."

"But that means..."

"I know what the fuck that means, but Cecilia doesn't have to know. Get the fucking details of the shipment and we'll see how it goes. Either way we need to use these docks or what the fuck do we have them for."

Ash nodded. "I'll let her know."

Grabbing his arm I held him back. "Be careful what you tell her. I don't trust her."

Ash glared at me and I could tell he was biting back a reply. "She's caught in the middle. You can't blame her for doing her job."

"You may be right, but make sure you're thinking with your head and not your dick when you're around her. Remember. One of your brothers is at stake here."

Ash hung his head and sighed. "Yes, Prez."

I slapped his back and he went back to her. I stayed out there for a long time, once again being pulled into the darkness. Cecilia would never forgive me if I put her life in danger, which meant I had to do everything in my power to make sure absolutely nothing went wrong with this job. Priscilla's words echoed in my head.

Nor do you want to be seen by those you are stealing from.

That thought made my gut wrench. Who were those men and why did I have a feeling there was more to this job than we were let onto? It wasn't just shipping items, it was a very well calculated operation. These items were worth millions of US dollars. What in the world had I gotten us into?

15

CECILIA

I'd woken up alone. Staring at the indent of his pillow. I couldn't believe he'd come into my room like that the night before. And on top of that he hadn't given me what we both so desperately wanted. Somehow, I was angry at him for that. Angry that he'd teased me, angry that I could cum so easily for him, angry that I had no control over my body when he was around.

He was the only man I'd ever been with and he knew it. It's why he took advantage of me, playing his fucking mind games. He could play all he wanted, I wasn't going to give into him. I was adamant about leaving. My heart wanted to stay, but every minute in this place only swallowed me back into the past. More bloodshed, more gunfire, more danger. He'd said La Plaga was dead, but for some reason I had a bad feeling in the pit of my stomach that told me that chapter of our story had not ended.

I made my way down to the kitchen and spotted Poe eating in the back booth. I smiled and slid in next to him, his grunt nearly made me laugh as he slid himself farther away from me.

"That looks good. Whatcha eatin'?" I liked teasing Poe, he was always so grumpy. I wondered how long it had been since he actually smiled. His chocolate eyes were soulful in their pain. And I had a soft spot for the big guy.

"What's it look like?" He eyed me for a second and then dug right back into his scrambled eggs and sausage. Cookie came over and set down a plate in front of me. A veggie omelet with a cup of coffee.

"Here you go sweetie. Poe, slow down, taste the damn food."

He grunted and continued to scarf down his food. She shook her head, a smile tugging at her lips. "This man is insufferable."

Winking at me, she turned and walked away, an extra bounce in her step. I eyed her, then I eyed him- cocking my head towards him.

"Cookie likes you."

He frowned and shrugged. "Yeah well, I don't like her."

"Aww, she's cute. There's nothing wrong with her, maybe there's something wrong with you?" I muttered under my breath.

He grunted in response. "Never said there was somethin' wrong with her. She's just too good for me, sweetheart. I don't do good. I do dirty."

I grimaced. "Ewww. Why are you so damn crude?"

"Cause it's the truth. Not every woman out there wants hearts and flowers and not every man is looking for a good girl."

I rolled my eyes at him and sunk into my fluffy omelet. Cookie had been with the club for a few years now. She did the cooking and helped Digger take care of the books. She had a thing for Poe, but I knew Digger had a thing for the pretty brunette. With all the women that roamed the club, you would think these boys would entertain them. There was no denying any one of them would kill to be a Death Row Shooter's Ol' Lady. The only one who seemed to indulge was Ash, but he only used them to satisfy his needs. Even Jayce, our Vindicator, had set his eyes on the pretty Brandy and God forbid if anyone touched her. His eyes were glued on that stage never leaving her. It was as if he were protecting her from something. Maybe even from himself.

How do I know all this? When you're stuck in a place this long without going out you start noticing things. These boys had an eternity of sleepless nights and needed to come home to a warm bed, yet they came home to nothing. A shame if you ask me. Because not only were these men mighty fine, they were the sort to take care of their women. If only they could step out of the darkness once in a while then maybe they wouldn't be so damn lonely.

"What's wrong with hearts and flowers?"

"That's not love, sweetheart. Loving is hard work, its rough, it's raw emotion. Hearts and flowers are bullshit."

"Yeah well, others seem to think that love is owning someone."

He turned to me then and scowled. "You think that man doesn't feel love for you?"

"I think he loves power more than he says he loves me."

"You want to talk about love, just look at his ridiculous face when you're around and you'll know exactly what I'm talking about. You're his fucking weakness and don't think we haven't noticed. We also don't like the idea of having a woman like you in the clubhouse."

"A woman like me?"

"You're a blind spot. We never saw you coming."

"It's not as easy as you picture it, Poe. He hurt me. Bad."

"So what?"

"What?" I looked at him as if he'd lost his head.

"He hurt you because he had to protect you. He didn't do it on purpose. Know the difference. You think he doesn't hurt? He ain't made of steel, as much as he thinks he is. That man's been hurtin' since the first day he was left without you. Remember that."

"He sure doesn't act that way," I murmured under my breath.

"Why? Cause he's not whispering empty promises in your ear and falling to his knees? He ain't about pretty shit, sweetheart. He's about loving hard and fast. The good kind of shit, ya know? The kind that lasts."

"It wasn't easy."

"For either of you. That boy has not had one moment of peace in his whole fucking life. He's the best man I know, the best fucking Prez I know, and my loyalty lies with him. I love you, doll, but if you hurt him you won't have my vote."

I looked at him for a long moment, watching as he gulped down his coffee. From what I knew, Poe had a hard life too. He came into the Death Row Shooters with hope and it had been torn away the day Nate died and then Simon. He'd found his brother in Ryan and I respected his loyalty. It meant he always had his back. What I didn't like was the fact that he made me feel like I was the bad guy in all this.

"You act like I came here to hurt him." His eyes were on me, a sharp glare in them. I looked right at him, not cowering, I'd done enough of that with my father around. "Don't ever forget who dragged me down here. We're both gluttons for punishment."

"You're both fools," he muttered and gulped down the rest of his coffee.

He slid out of the seat, but before he left he got his last word in. "Love ain't easy, Cecilia. It takes work and heart. If you're not willing to do that, then let him go."

I looked up at him and blinked. "Don't you get it Poe? I already let go. He's the one that keeps bringing me back."

He hung his head knowing I was right. "Then it's on him. The heart has to suffer, just don't make him suffer to badly."

He walked away, and I stared at his slumped shoulders. There was a reason he was called the Poet, but it wasn't because of his fists, he was definitely poetic in matters of the heart too. I was certain that any woman who was able to get close to that man- would be loved to every extremity.

I swallowed down the rest of my eggs in silence and when done I slid out of booth and made my way down the hallway. Ryan was coming out of a back room when I approached, and instantly I pulsed, remembering the feel of him between my legs.

I wanted to run past him and hide, but there was no hiding from a man who was determined to make me his. As soon as I swept past him, he swept a hand around me and pressed me up against the wall.

"No good morning?"

"I'm not in the mood," I placed my hands on his chest trying to squirm out of his hold. He felt so damn good I thought I'd melt right there.

"I like when you struggle against me, Firefly," he nipped at my ear. "Makes me fucking hard as fuck for you."

I whimpered as he sucked on my earlobe showing me just how hard he was.

"I'm sorry I left you so early this morning. I wanted to finish what we started."

"There's nothing to finish because it was a mistake."

He cocked his head to the side and narrowed his eyes on me. "Go out with me?"

"What?"

"Come on, we'll go for a ride."

"I have things to do," I stated as he grabbed my hand and tugged me down the hallway.

"Come on, Firefly, I know you ain't got shit to do."

I rolled my eyes but followed him out obediently. His old Harley stood out front and he handed me a helmet right before he revved up the bike.

I took him in for a second. Leather jacket, expensive slacks, thousand-dollar shiny black boots, and black aviator sunglasses that covered his eyes. He looked dangerous and sexy sitting on his throne. He turned to me and I felt his heated gaze on me, quickly I slid in behind him.

Grabbing my knee as he always did, we took off. I didn't bother asking where we were going, he wasn't going to tell me anyway.

I WALKED DOWN TO THE WATER'S EDGE, THE SUN glistened on the small crescent waves that lapped along the rock ridden path. He'd brought me here before, years ago, on his birthday. That was the day he'd promised to always stay by my side. A bittersweet memory now. I could sense him a few feet away, his eyes on me, always on me as he leaned against his bike.

"Are you coming?" I looked back at him and he smiled, heading down the path towards me.

We walked quietly to that one spot, the log still hidden on the curve of the path. Our own secluded spot where no one was ever able to find us. Holding my hand, he helped me up first and then he sat himself down next to me.

Grabbing my hand, he laced his fingers through mine. The touch was warm, sending tingles up my arm. We sat in silence for a long time, watching the sun begin to set. He was the first one to speak. "I don't like this, Cecilia. I don't like what we've become."

I didn't say anything, just played with the leather band of his bracelet.

"I want to make this right. How do I fix this? Fix us?"

"There's no fixing us, Ryan. We were broken from the start."

"That's not true."

"But it is. I don't think this was ever meant to be."

"Horse shit!"

He yanked his hand away and leapt off the log. I watched him pace back and forth, he looked like a caged panther readying himself to be released into the wild. When he looked at me, I shivered.

"Why are you so fucking stubborn?"

"Why are you so damn arrogant?" I jumped off the log and walked up the path. "Let's go, I'm done here."

Grabbing my arm, he whirled me around. "We go when I say we go."

"It's always your way, isn't it? It's my life, Ryan. Mine! I won't let you take that away from me and I don't take orders from anyone, least of all you."

I jerked my arm away and walked back towards his bike. I knew it held sentimental value to him. Simon had sent him that bike the night he'd died. He never took it out anymore, and somehow, the fact that he'd let me ride on it today made my heart melt for him.

Grabbing me, he whirled me around to face him. His

heated breath on my face as he seethed in anger. God how he looked gorgeous angry, like a wild beast about to let himself loose on me. The masochist in me loved it, the submissive begged to be put on her knees, but the woman in me wanted to run.

"Don't you dare fucking blame me for what happened! Your life was on the line, I did what was best!"

"You don't get it do you?"

"There's nothing to get, Cecilia. I know what I did was right."

"You were everything to me, Ryan. All I had." I swallowed down the lump in my throat. It was no use to cry anymore.

"Cecilia, I..."

"And you left me. Just like that."

"I came back!"

"You have no idea what it means to lose everything! To lose your freedom! And now what, you think you own me?"

"I don't, do I? You want to know what it means to lose your freedom, sweetheart." His hands reached out to me, capturing me against him. I punched at his chest, but he only squeezed me tighter, forcing me to still.

"I'm so fucking done with your attitude! I'm going to show you what it means to be owned by the Death Row Shooters, Cecilia. And when I'm done with you, you'll regret denying me anything."

"I'm not..." I gasped, losing my words as he twirled me around, bending me over the bike. "Ryan!" I cried out as he spanked me over my leggings, his growl of frustration heating up my loins and forced little whimpers from me.

"Fuck, those whimpers make my cock hard for you, Cecilia." His rough tone matched the grinding of his pelvis on my ass.

"I was sweet with you last night, but today I'm done. You want to fuck with me, then let's fuck!"

My head jerked at the sound of that familiar click, the sound made my core clench. Turning, I watched as he lay the blade flat on my skin. That damn blade he always kept on him. I used to watch him play around with that blade, flinging it against the wall. He was lethal with it, an extension of his hand, and now that blade was on me. His eyes met mine as he tilted it up, the sharp edge now gliding down the crevice of my ass.

"Ryan," my tone was a mixture of need and fear.

What if he nicked me? What if I bled? What if I liked it? God, I was fucked up.

He gripped the stretchy material of my leggings and in seconds he had it split it in two, gaining access to my flesh. I held my breath as he ran the blade along the crevice of my right thigh, and then my left. Turning it, he brushed the flat of the steel along my wet lips, slightly tapping at it as I quivered in anticipation. He was playing with me, a sinful game, and if he wasn't careful he could hurt me.

Hurt me? Ryan would never hurt me.

I whimpered as I felt the tip of the blade run across the seam of my panties, the only article keeping my core out of his reach. I held my breath and clenched my eyes shut, unexpectedly there was a forceful tug, and I screamed as my panties were ripped off me.

Running his rough palms across my ass, he squeezed and groaned. That damn groan sending a needy thrill down my spine. Expertly, he slid the edge of the knife along my pussy lips, along the curve that met my thigh. It felt so fucking good, that damn sharp point teasing me, my pussy pulsing and becoming so damn slick.

"I'm going to cum, Ryan."

His hand came down on me and he hissed. "What did I tell you before?"

I whimpered in need. "I cum when you tell me to cum."

I gripped the leather seat and bit my lip, the game he was playing was daring, and I held myself still trying to keep my breath steady so that the blade wouldn't cut through me. Oddly, I found the idea erotic and I moaned as the tip of the blade outlined my heart shaped ass.

"You have a fine ass, baby. It makes my cock itch to watch it jiggle as I fuck it hard." He gripped my hair and yanked my head back against his shoulder. "Because I will be fucking you tonight, Angel. Long and hard. I want that fire you have licking at my cock. Your cock."

I gasped as he spanked me and knelt once again behind me, rubbing his beard along my sensitive skin, his hot breath skimming along the cheek, the blade gliding up along the flesh of my ass-circling the globe. He smacked my inner thighs, forcing to spread my legs open, the knife cutting off more of the stretchy material. He yanked at the silk of my panties and threw them in the air. I stared at them as they clung to the handle of the motorcycle, torn to shreds.

"Those were my fav-" I squealed as he spanked me and bit down hard on my fleshy cheek. He was rough tonight, more than I thought he would be, but I wanted it. I wanted him like this.

"Fuck," I groaned as his tongue dragged from the entrance of my wet pussy and twirled against my asshole. Over and over, he growled and moaned as he had me for a fucking meal. His tongue curling and lapping, sucking on me until my legs began to shake. I hung on to the seat of the bike, going up on tiptoes, gasping for breath as he sucked on my clit. Rapid, incessant strokes of his tongue bringing me to the edge.

"Ryan!" I cried out as he took a hard pull of my sensitive bud. His lips smacking as he popped it out of his mouth only to slurp it back up. I sank back onto him, my body gyrating as he fucked me on his tongue.

He pulled back and I moaned from the loss of him. "My own personal slut, rubbing this delicious sexy pussy on my beard." He rubbed his fingers against my slit, sliding along my juices and capturing my clit between them while squeezing. He took my breath away, a moan ripping from my throat while I ran my hands across my breasts and threw my head back in ecstasy. I didn't care anymore, I just wanted to get lost in him.

"Help me, Ryan. Make me forget," I whimpered as he dove right back in, sucking and nibbling on my most sensitive area. He grunted as he bit softly on the flesh of my thighs. I flung myself forward, spreading my thighs as far as they'd go. I felt like a needy slut on display and I didn't give a fuck. If this is how he wanted me then this is how he'd have me.

His tongue delved into my core, lapping away at the entrance of my pussy hole and I whined, pushing back on him, my body begging for more.

He spanked me hard and my legs shook. "You want to be my dirty little whore, don't you?" He growled, and I swear my pussy leaked. I bent far over, stretching my back, my mouth gaped open as I watched him between my legs. I watched as a drop of my juices drooled down and he caught it on his wet tongue. It clung to him as he savored it.

"That sweet pussy's dripping honey," the rich timbre in his voice mixed with the pad of his thumb circling my clit made me cry out.

"You want to cum?" He pressed down firmly on my clit and I squirmed on him.

"Y-yes. Yes please."

He spanked me again and I yelled out in need. "Not until I goddamn tell you to!"

He stood up, leaving me, and I whimpered, wanting more. Leaning over me I raised a shoulder as his beard tickled my neck. "Straddle the bike, Cecilia."

The hard edge in his tone made me shiver. This was not the boy I left behind, this was all man. The Reaper was stealing my soul tonight and I wasn't going to stop him.

On shaky legs I managed to hike a leg up on the bike, spreading myself wide before I slid on. My pussy rubbed wickedly against the leather sending shocks down my legs. He shook his jacket off beside me and hung it on the handle bar. Gripping my hair, he leaned into me, dragging his tongue along my lips. He tasted of pussy juice and mint and I sucked on his tongue, greedy for more. With the tip of the knife he outlined my lips.

"Such pretty pink lips. I'm gonna make you beg now, Cecilia."

Pushing my head forward, he climbed on the back of the bike behind me. I could hear the pull of his zipper, his groan as he released himself. I looked back and grabbing my head, he forced it forward. His touch was gentle but firm, and I obeyed. "Grip the handles."

I leaned forward slightly, my pussy soaking the leather seat. I gripped the handles and he moaned as he stroked my exposed ass. He slapped it and I jumped slightly, the sting hot and achingly good.

"Now stand on the stirrups, Cecilia."

"Yes, Sir," I breathed, and he grunted in approval.

"Look at the mess you've made, Cecilia. Such a dirty pussy deserves to get punished." He slid closer on the seat and gripped my hips. The tip of his cock played along my wet slit, and my whole body quivered in need. His hands came around my breasts, massaging the aching buds and he growled as I leaned back, perched on the stirrups.

"No bra?"

"Uh-uh," I panted, and he hissed as he yanked my t-shirt up, the soft breeze caressing my nipples. My cry was a mixture of pleasure and need as he slid his rough hands along my plump tits, softly kneading the soft mounds and pinching the tips.

"Fucking tease," his deep rumble had me pressing back onto him. "You feel so fucking good, you know that?"

The swollen head of his dick played at my entrance and I leaned my head against his shoulder, waiting. He lifted slightly, entering me at a painstakingly slow pace. The crown of his cock brushing against the sensitive spot just inside my entrance.

"Ryan." I breathed his name, a plea that got lost in the silence of the evening.

The blade was suddenly pressed to my throat and as I swallowed I could feel the edge of it pushing against me. I shivered while his grip tightened on my hair, tugging it back.

"If you want my dick you need to beg for it."

"Fuck me. Please."

"You want to get fucked, Cecilia. Your pussy's swollen and needy for me, isn't it?"

He swept his hands across my clit and I yelled out. "Yes! God, yes!"

"Do it," he whispered huskily in my ear and my body arched back. With a loud moan I slid down his thick shaft, feeling it stretch me as it entered me, that familiar sweet ache palpitating between my thighs.

"Oh!" I cried out as he shoved me forward, the tip of the

blade sliding gently down the sides of my spine as his hips moved against me.

"Ride me, Firefly. Grip the handles and ride yourself to that sweet freedom you yearn for so badly."

"Fuck," I whimpered as I leaned forward, his cock penetrating me deep. He hissed and spanked my ass again as I started to move on him. My body rocking back onto his dick, my legs weak from the delicious friction. He wanted me to fuck him, to use his body to get off. It was the hottest thing I'd ever heard, and my pussy ached as it dripped on him. Up and down, I dropped my hips, wriggling down and crying out as he spanked me. My tits swayed while my pussy clenched down on him.

"That's a good girl, ride that cock. That's your cock." He grunted and lifted his hips, fucking me right back. "If you want your freedom, you'll have to take me with you."

I cried out as his thrusts got deeper and our fucking got louder. The echo of our wet bodies slapping against each other would be audible along the lakeside, but we didn't care. We were lost in our own world. A world we'd created.

His hand swept down my back, his cock straining while my pussy tugged on it, rocking my body up and down his thick rod. His grunts heated my body, the fact that I could tear those sounds from him gave me all the reasons I needed to give myself to him.

"You're perfect for me, baby."

He swept his hand around my hips and dipped his fingers through my swollen slit. "Fuck, you're so damn horny for me. You missed me that much, Firefly?"

"Ohhh," my head flung back as his teeth nipped at my collar bone. His fingers flicked my clit and his tongue roamed the muscle that ran up the back of my neck.

"Cum for me, baby. Do it now," he growled in my ear

and the deep timbre of his command made my pussy spasm on him.

The orgasm was sweet as he rubbed the spot between my clit and what he called his honey hole. He knew just what to do to make me lose control. The pleasure took my breath away, not that he gave me much time to enjoy it. Lifting me into his arms, he lay me down on the bike, grabbing handfuls of my breasts as he looked me over, outlining my body. He slid the leggings off me and kissed my tummy, licking a path along my hip bones.

"You're mine, Firefly. You belong to the President of the Death Row Shooters and your only escape is to put a bullet in me."

My breath hitched as he placed a kiss on my clit. He grabbed my thighs and slid me down carefully to the edge of the seat, standing on the stirrups, his cock was aimed at my center. I pulsed in excitement and with an audible hiss of pleasure, he slid right into the depths of me. I don't think any man could ever make me feel this complete. His first thrust made me cry out, the second made me sigh, and thrust after thrust of his hips had me gyrating against him and begging him to be rougher with my body.

"You'll have to do better than that if you want me to feel you buried inside of me tomorrow."

He roared and punished me, his hands squeezing the flesh of my ass as he guided me onto his thickness. It felt so damn good-I fought not to scream.

He swept his thumb across my clit and my stomach muscles clenched while I fought the desire threatening to unravel in me. Hot, tempting liquid heat ran across my tummy as his thumb just made deep circles against me.

"You're so fucking beautiful," that damn timbre of his voice did things to my insides. "I want to own every fucking inch of your body, baby." Sliding his hand up my body, he grabbed at my tits, playing with the tips just like he had my clit. A direct line of pleasure either way as he pinched and flicked, and then he leaned over me and bit down on me, my body arching against him, offering itself to him. His cock throbbing between my legs as he continued a slow fuck that made me wetter than I was before.

"I can feel your pussy, baby. It likes to get fucked by your President. By your owner." I moaned in heat as his words were like triggers that enticed every nerve ending that travelled to my core.

"That little pussy's going to cum on my dick, isn't it? Mmngh, I got it all juicy, just for me."

"Ryan," I whined as he fucked me just a little bit harder. His thrusts getting faster, the angle hitting that sweet g spot. My legs lifted, my toes curl, and arching my back I shouted as the orgasm tore through me.

"Fuck, Ryan!"

"Fuck," he groaned in my ear and I looked up at the night sky while he filled me with his liquid heat. Long pulls of cum that pumped into me. His hot breath came out in ragged grunts that tickled my neck. I pressed my cheek to his, cooing at him as his body slowly calmed, the sound of crickets surrounding us.

He turned his head to look at me. "You belong to me, Cecilia. You always have. Don't ever fucking forget that."

I shuddered as he pulled out of me, and the cool air swept over me as he pulled us off of the bike. He threw the leather jacket at me and frowned. "Put that on. Zipper it all the way up, I don't want anyone looking at what's mine."

The jacket was bulky, and it fell down mid-thigh. I stared down at my bare legs and looked at him. He arched a brow. "It'll do. Let's go. I gotta get you back home. I have shit to do."

I swallowed the lump that had formed in my throat as I slid along the back of the bike. The Harley roared to life and I whimpered in his ear, my exposed pussy aching from the deep rumble of the V-Twin engine. He gripped my knee and hung his head for a moment. The grip was tight on me, reassuring me in a sense. He was still mad at me, but I didn't dare say anything. I clung to him as he swept the bike around and headed back down the mountain. It was dark, so no one would see a half-naked woman perched on the back of the bike of the most notorious bikers in Sacramento, California. And even if they did, they'd keep their mouths shut and their eyes forward, because I was Reaper property, and no one fucked with what was his.

After a long ride, he helped me off the bike, and without a word he took my hand and walked us into the lobby of the Den. But as we walked in, he froze. Looking around his shoulder I noticed that the Death Row Shooters had very unexpected visitors.

"Go get changed," Ryan stated, his back tense, his stance ready to fight.

"Ryan, I..."

"I said go get changed!"

I flinched when he yelled and slowly backed away. I heard Wolf's voice as I crept up the stairs and towards the apartment.

"It's obvious why we're here, Reaper."

I watched Ryan run a hand through his beard. "Fuck my life."

The words he uttered couldn't have weighed more heavily on my heart. Having the Hellbound Lovers here meant that Ryan was in trouble. I was under their protection and as much as I appreciated it, I didn't want Ryan paying the consequences. I realized then that I was never truly free. Not how I was at that lake a few hours ago. I always belonged to someone, and at this point, I'd rather belong to Ryan than anyone else.

16

CECILIA

"We know she's not here under her own free will, Reaper. We want her back."

"Over my dead body."

"That can be arranged," Grayson was toe to toe with Ryan. The energy in the room was electric, one wrong move and I was sure someone was going to die.

"She was happy, Ryan. Don't you realize that?" Wolf's statement couldn't have rung truer. He knew what I'd gone through, how I'd suffered. He was the only one who knew it all.

"I will not give her up," Ryan seethed, the muscles on his neck straining. He was adamant on keeping me and in a way that connection was all I needed, and in another, it was stifling. I was confused, torn. I wanted my freedom, but I wanted it with him.

"Well you're going to have to! Carlos Trejo was seen hanging out by the docks."

Ryan's face changed, his eyes going wide in surprise. "That's impossible!"

"Brother, when have you known Riggs to be wrong in

his intel? He's out there, he confirmed it. We've known for a few days now."

"My own man put a bullet in him!" Ryan yelled.

Grayson nodded. "He may have put a bullet in him, but he didn't kill him. That fucker is alive."

My hand wrapped around my throat, the mention of his name gave me chills. He said he'd always come back for me. Even the dead were rising to haunt us.

"Ash wouldn't lie to me! He was shot and killed." Ryan turned away from Wolf and Grayson and the look in his eyes said it all. *Betrayal.*

"Someone died that night, Ryan. We know that for a fact because Ash asked for our help. We couldn't make it that night and instead the Devil's Syndicate rode over. Word is they buried a body, just not the right one."

"Goddammit!" Ryan shouted flinging his chair against the wall.

"He'd been gone for a long time, it's easy to have mistaken him for someone else."

"Ash doesn't make mistakes."

"We all make mistakes." Wolf's statement hung heavy in the silence.

"We're the only ones who can protect her and you damn well know it."

"I'm the only one! *Me*! I won't let you take her again! Not again," he screamed as he met Grayson's dark glare.

"Don't I have a say?" My voice rang loud and clear in the quiet space.

Ryan turned and narrowed his eyes. "Go back upstairs, Cecilia. This does not concern you."

"The hell it doesn't!" I narrowed my eyes on each and every one of them. All big burly men who became blushing fools as I challenged them. Wolf and Grayson at least had the decency to look down, ashamed, but not Ryan. He met my glare head on, his own lust filled challenge in his eyes. He liked me this way, fired up, I could feel it.

"Go back," he whispered, carefully approaching me. Careful not to startle me. He reached for me, but I dodged his touch and that only infuriated him more. Raising a hand, I placed it on his chest and he only stood there, staring down at it. Any other woman or man would have removed it, I simply lay it there, right over his heart. He met my eyes and wrapped his hands around mine. His eyes were full of anguish and I almost got lost in their storm.

"She's right, Reaper. She has every right to be here, it's her decision. Stay or go."

I couldn't keep my eyes off Ryan and I knew if I let him, he'd hold onto me as long as he could. The question was, did I want him to let me go?

"Leave us," he stated, and I could hear Wolf and Grayson shuffling.

"Ryan, stop being so goddamn hard headed!" Wolf has always been the voice of reason and I always looked up to him. He'd been my caretaker for so long, if there was anyone I could trust it was him.

"Wolf." I looked over at him and he understood.

Wolf took a deep breath. "You have five minutes. You got that Ryan?"

"Get out," he growled.

As soon as the door slammed behind us Ryan's hands wrapped around my waist. "Don't go."

My heartbeat was racing as his warmth engulfed me. He was once again sharing all that vulnerability with me. I could feel it in his hands, the desperation. It overwhelmed me.

"Why?" My voice was surprisingly calm.

"Because you're mine."

"Says who? You?" Sarcasm dripped from my voice, but I didn't care. I was tired of being manipulated and considered an object instead of a woman. I was a goddamn human being and he will treat me as such.

"Fuck, yes! And you goddamn know it's true. You're mine in every way."

"Cause I let you put your dick in me a few hours ago? You think you own me because I made you hard, because you made me cum? Don't be ridiculous. You have another thing coming Reaper if you think that's enough to own someone!"

His eyes met mine and he pushed at my waist, shoving me until I was pressed against the back wall, I could see the anger simmering in his eyes, and the wheels turning in his head.

"You like to corner weak animals, don't you? That's all you know how to do!"

"Stop it!" He shouted making me squeeze my eyes shut as his hands cupped my mouth.

I wrapped my fingers around his wrists and brought them down. "You think you owe me something, you don't owe me anything, Ryan. I don't want anything from you!"

"Me!" He banged at his chest, hard.

I paused for a moment, not really understanding what he was trying to say. "What?"

"I owe you me. My life. It's yours."

I blinked slowly, trying to capture what he was saying to me. His confession made my heart race once again. He had this way of manipulating this weak heart of mine to be at his beck and call and somehow, I both hated and loved that. But this time it felt like it was going to leap out of my throat.

"You can't do that," I breathed.

"What? Is that too much for you to handle. You'll let me stick my cock in you, take what I want from you and fill me with your sweet moans, but my feelings are too much for you."

I shook my head. "I don't want you."

"Lies!" His head rocked from side to side while pressed against my forehead. His hands on my cheeks tightening. "You're fucking lying to me," He whispered, the sadness in his voice tore at me. His dark eyes met mine and I shivered. "Do you know why I know this?"

I slowly shook my head, afraid to voice my own feelings.

He gave a slight smirk and closed his eyes. "Because of the way you feel in my arms," he squeezed them for reassurance. "That deep shudder that runs through you as you give yourself to me, as if you know that's where you belong. Perched on my cock and wrapped around me."

"Ryan." I warned, a deep blush seeping into my cheeks.

"You wanted me. Don't deny it." He held me tight as I let a breath out.

"I never did. I won't deny I want you, I do. But not like this." His nostrils flared, and his jaw clenched as I spoke the words.

"I don't give a shit what you want anymore. I'm fucking done playing games. I left you once, I won't do it again."

"You have to let me go. He's out there! Somehow he survived. You know Wolf's right. He'll find me if you don't."

"I want him to!" He screamed and slammed a hand on the wall to my right. His other hand roamed down my top, slowly caressing the tops of my breasts as he hung his head. "I want him to find you," he whispered.

When his eyes finally met mine, I knew he wasn't going to let me go, and I knew it was pointless to fight him, but that wouldn't stop me. "You're crazy."

He narrowed his gaze on me, reaching into his pocket. "If he dares to come looking for you, I'll make sure this bullet goes right through his head and stays there, just like I said it would that night."

I shivered from the dark edge held in his tone. This wasn't the boy that left me, this wasn't the man who I let between my thighs last night. This. This was The Reaper, hard edged, cold blooded, calculating murderer.

"More blood? I can't do this anymore, Ryan."

"Would you rather I let him live?" He searched my face for a long moment and I knew the answer.

"Maybe he should just go to jail." I tried, but I knew that wasn't the answer he was searching for.

He smirked and hung his head. "You're a fool, Cecilia. I never took you for a fool."

"I want this death toll to stop."

"Then it stops with him," he seethed.

"Either way, you can't keep me here. You already kidnapped me once, you're lucky Wolf hasn't called the cops on you."

"Yeah, I doubt he'll do that. Besides he has connections in the FBI and CIA, you think he wouldn't have called them already. He's waiting on me. It's my move and he knows it." He turned to leave, and I clutched his hand in mine.

"Ryan, please. Please let me go." I begged him even though I already knew the answer. I was trapped in between two men, the one I loved, and the one I didn't know.

He turned to me, his jaw clenched tight. "Stop now, Cecilia. I'll never let anyone hurt you."

"You're hurting me!" I yelled back at him. As soon as the words spilled off my tongue he came at me, his hard body molding to mine as he pressed me up against the wall.

My nipples instinctively reacted, hardening in the light tank top I wore. He looked down and smiled as he dragged his palms up my sides and wrapped his hands around them. I watched, taking shallow breaths, as his thumbs stroked my hardened nipples. My breath caught as he held my gaze, my cheeks flushed, my breathing unsteady. This is how he wanted me, vulnerable and willing to do anything for his touch.

"I'll never hurt you," he pinched my nipples and I whimpered. "Unless you want me to."

"Ryan," I breathed as his knee pressed between my thighs forcing me to straddle him. My pussy grinding involuntarily onto his muscled thigh while his hands dragged the straps of my tank off my shoulders.

"Cause I can make you hurt, sweetheart. So good," he growled as he yanked the tank down exposing my breasts. "God, these tits are so fucking perfect."

I cried out as he bit down on the top curve of my breast. Like the wild animal that he was, he was marking me, and my body instinctively reacted to his mouth on me. He held me tight as my hips went wild along his slacked covered thigh. My panties were drenched from the exquisite friction.

His tongue flicked and circled my nipple, sucking on it before he ran it up along my neck, nipping at the soft flesh of my earlobe. "I want you hot, fired up, angry. I want you to fight me, Angel. Fight."

I cried out as his hands pinched my nipples, my hands grabbing at the lapels of his expensive suit. "When they're gone, I'm going to tie you up to my bed and lap at your cunt until you're crying my name. I want you to scream it, do you hear me? I want you to claw at my back as I fuck you into submission."

"Fuck," I breathed. And just as quickly as he'd cornered me, he backed away.

I missed him instantly, my body wanting to be connected to his. He watched me for a long moment, my breasts heaving, taught nipples, red marks where he bit me. His hand went down to the crotch of his pants and he gripped his cock, the outline of it making my pussy clench.

"I'll be back for you, sweet Cecilia. My cock is in need of your body."

"Ryan. Please." I shuddered as he took a step closer, the heat from his body making me sway into him. Grabbing my arms, he held me slightly away from him.

"You're mine. Mine to protect, mine to fuck, mine to keep. That's the last of it. If you go against the rules that the President of the Death Row Shooters has set in place, you'll get punished Cecilia."

He let go of me and walked towards the door. With his back turned, he spoke to me. "I won't lock the door, Firefly. But don't force me to go to extremes for you."

I tried to assimilate everything that had just happened. I had a feeling going with the Hellbound Lovers would start a war but staying with Ryan would wreak havoc on my soul. The decision was made to spill more blood, and I could do nothing to stop it. All I could do was pray that it wasn't Ryan's blood that would spill in my hands this time around.

17

RYAN

My mind was blurred with thoughts of Cecilia as I finished up with Wolf and Grayson. Well, more like sent them on their way.

"We'll be back for her, Reaper." Wolf stated before turning and walking out. I could tell he was livid, but I also knew he understood where I came from. He was giving me a chance not to fuck this up.

Cecilia was my crutch, in every way possible. I wanted to protect her, but in this case, I was going to have to make the right decision. Just not yet. I just needed a little more time. Reaching Ash's door, I ripped it open and barged in. Ash was standing by the window; his cock being sucked on by one of the club whores. She slowly sucked him out, a stream of her spit clung to the head of his cock.

"What the fuck, man?" Ash yelled out, not giving a shit about standing there butt naked.

"Get the fuck out," I roared and the whore scrambled to her feet, grabbed her clothes and ran out.

Ash gave me an icy glare as he slipped on his briefs followed by his jeans. "This better be fucking urgent."

"You fucking traitor!"

I charged at him and slammed him up against the window, my forearm pressed to his neck. "You said you killed him."

"What the fuck are you talking about, kid?" Ash's eyes shown in confusion and he grunted as I put pressure on his jugular.

"He's alive." I muttered, shaking in fury as a deadly stillness filled the air.

Ash gripped my arm and shook his head. "Impossible. I put a bullet in him."

"Liar! You fucking betrayed me!" I forced my arm against his throat and the sound of him choking on his own tongue brought me a great deal of satisfaction.

"I swear on my son, Brother. I know I put a bullet through him."

The words meant something to Ash, his son meant the world to him, he would never swear so easily on his family. Not on the ones he loved beyond life itself. Not if he was telling the truth. Slowly, I removed my arm and stood before him, still angry, the mere idea of being betrayed had me on edge.

"Talk," I seethed.

He coughed and sputtered, before looking at me. "You would have killed me?"

"I said fucking talk!" I took a step towards him, clenching my fists to keep myself from doing him any more harm.

Holding his hands up he started to speak. "I did what I said I would do that night. I got the call from La Mancha letting me know that Carlos Trejo was back and if I wanted dibs."

La Mancha was the leader of La Sombra, a gang that

was part of the Mexican Mafia. They were notorious for sex trafficking, drug and weapon trafficking, and god knows what the fuck else. Out of the hundreds of gangs that existed in Los Angeles, La Mancha took a liking to us. We helped launder his money, he had our backs. No gang was allowed in Death Row Shooter territory without La Mancha's permission. Luckily, we were both after the same man. When La Mancha came knocking on our door he was looking for Carlos Trejo. Motherfucker had knocked up his sixteen-year-old daughter and he was out for his head. Son of a bitch ran away before Ash could find him and bring me my justice. Out of respect to us, La Mancha called a few months ago. It was a free for all, whoever got to him first would keep his head. Unfortunately, we got the wrong head.

Ash continued to speak. "I chased the fucker down Folsom, but he was fast. I caught up as he took the highway up to the mountains, finally getting a clear shot. I saw him topple down the mountain, Ryan! I fucking buried him!"

He wasn't lying, I could see it in his eyes. He was adamant that he'd shot him. "How do you know it was him?"

"It was his bike, Brother. My bike!"

The souped up Harley used to belong to Ash until Mario took it from him and handed it to that piece of shit VP of his. Ash had been devastated, but Simon said he'd get it back sooner or later. Unfortunately, he never got a chance to go through with his word. But the bike had somehow returned as Death Row Shooters property, after La Plaga was supposedly shot, and Ash had taken back what was his. Bringing back the bike was more than enough proof that he had gotten his man.

"I buried him," he shook his head.

"Are you sure it was him?"

He shook his head. "I can't tell you that." He ran his hand across his dark scruff. "It was so fucking dark out there. We buried him deep, if not the coyotes would have ripped him to pieces and scattered him all over the fucking mountains."

"How the flying fuck did he get away?"

"I don't know. But I shot and killed somebody that night and he was wearing a Death Row Shooters patch, but he wasn't one of ours."

"Find out who's fucking buried in that hole!"

He nodded and swept past me, grabbing his boots and leathers. I stared out the window, the morning sun highlighted the worn-down sidewalks of Sacramento, California. My whole had come crumbling down in seconds with the fucking news of La Plaga's survival. I couldn't keep her here. It was too dangerous.

What the fuck was I going to do?

I turned and walked back to my office, thoughts of Cecilia still running through my head. I could still feel her hesitation, even after all that. But I was going to teach her she can't live without me. By the end of it, she was going to beg me to stay with her.

Why the fuck was I so damn selfish?

Why the fuck was I such a fuck up?

I walked into the office and there she was, looking through my mess of papers and invoices. I wanted to hear her beg for me again, but this time I wanted to be lodged deep inside of that tight little pussy as she pleaded for me. I loved how she trembled, those tits bouncing on that sweet body of hers as she came for me. She was eager for me last night and as much as she wanted to fight it, she loved every second of it.

"What the hell are you doing?"

"Look at this mess. You're so unorganized." She held up a stack of bills and I leaned forward and snapped them out of her hand.

"That's none of your fucking business."

"Why, cause it's club business?" She stood and walked around the desk, propping her pretty ass on the edge of it.

"I'm glad you're here, we need to talk."

"If it's about last night you can forget about it. It was a mistake. It won't ever happen again."

"A mistake? It didn't feel like a mistake, especially when you screamed my name as your tight little pussy came for me over and over again."

"Why do you have to be so crude?"

"You blush like a virgin," my dark gaze narrowed on her.

"There's no denying I found pleasure in what we did last night, but that doesn't mean anything."

"Why do you lie to yourself? The fact that you let me in, that you let me touch you, it meant everything to me. Why take that away from me? And as much as you deny it, I know you want me as much as I want you. Maybe even a little more."

The sexy little vixen smirked at me. "You're delusional."

"Am I," I pulled at the waistband of her shorts and pressed my hard cock against her.

"There's no need to fight me, Cecilia. All I want is to give you pleasure. Let me give you what I can, sweet girl."

"Ryan, please," her moan got lost in my mouth as I swept my lips across hers. My tongue flicked at her top lip and she gasped as it slid its way through and mated with hers. It was a seductive dance, one that showed my devotion to her, my love for her. She gave in easily as I overpowered her senses in every way I could.

"I can't keep myself from you. I need you." I rumbled against her lips as I slowly tasted her. Holding her tightly, I ran kisses down the side of her neck drawing out shivers as I played with the strap of her tank top.

"I want to see your needy breasts. Lick and bite them and make you cum from my mouth on them alone." My murmurs drew out long sexy sighs. I dragged my tongue along the top curve of her breast, biting down on the tip and she cried out her pleasure.

"Is your dirty little pussy drenched for me, Cecilia? Do you need my cock?"

She moaned, and my cock pulsed at the sound. Running my hands down her waist, my fingers stopped at the button of her shorts. "Take them off."

"No," she whispered harshly, a defiant look in her eyes. "You want this, take them off your goddamn self."

"You want to play this game Cecilia? Cause I'll force my cock so deep inside I will guarantee you will feel it the next day, and the day after." I growled angrily as I unsnapped the button. My eyes never left her challenging ones as I yanked down those damn shorts that tempted the fuck out of me.

Shoving her back onto the desk, she cried out from the roughness of my actions. She tried to kick at me, but I grabbed her knees and forced them apart. Her glistening swollen lips appeared, and my cock throbbed at the lack of underwear.

"Fuck, you're so beautiful. Did you come here prepared for me, Angel? Your pussy all juicy and ready for my tongue?"

Before she could breathe a word, my mouth was on her, those sexy little whimpers making my cock swell and grow heavy. I undid the zipper of my pants, pulling myself out as I had her creaminess swirling on my tongue.

"Such a dirty little slut made just for me."

I lifted my head, her cum on my beard and lips as I slid my cock through her wet folds. I licked at my lips hungrily and she whimpered for me. "I want to fuck you with the taste of your dirty pussy on my tongue."

"Oh my, God," her breath caught as I slipped my thick head into heated walls, I had to thrust a little to insert myself into her depths. Throwing her head back as I molded her pussy to my cock.

"That's right, baby. You will worship no other god but me." I slid out and thrust deep, fucking her hard as she cried out my name. Her cunt tightened around my dick so good, my groans were hers and hers alone. I utterred her name under my breath while I tilted my hips and drove myself deep inside of her warm pussy.

I enjoyed taking her breath away, the feeling of being consumed by her was like heaven. It made me swell and ache for more. She felt so soft against me, so eager, and she was slowly coming to the conclusion that she was mine whenever I fucking wanted her. On that first stroke, she tensed, but it felt so fucking good penetrating her. I couldn't help but do it again and again. In the dim lights I watched her face, a frown on her brow, a tremble along her bottom lip. She may not like me right now, but she was going to accept what I wanted to give to her.

"You belong to me now, Angel," I roared as I began to fuck her hard up against that desk. Her cries were both of pleasure and pain and I knew I was stretching her to her limit. I was a big man, far thicker and longer than most, and he was so damn tight as her velvet silk clamped onto my dick.

Pre-cum flowed between us as I continued to pump into her. She whimpered in my ear and I lifted her in the air- my cock still sliding in and out of her as I lifted her up and down on it. Slamming us both up against the wall, I dug in deeper. My body completely trapping hers as our bodies gyrated against one another. Her sweet little pussy clinging to me as rippled purrs escaped those pouty lips. Ripping the rest of her tank off, I engulfed a tit in my mouth, biting down on it to leave my mark.

I slowed down just enough to allow her to feel how good my cock stretched her, how every inch sank in deeper and deeper, claiming her. I rolled my hips against her in such a heated embrace, her legs shook and she bit her lip trying to keep from crying out her pleasure.

"Cum for me, Cecilia. Claim my cock like you have my heart."

"Ryan!" She screamed as the orgasm tore through her, taking her precious breath away.

I roared out my pent-up lust for her as my body tensed and loads of hot cum coated the walls of her womb.

18

CECILIA

I SCREAMED as the door flew off its hinges bringing me down to the floor. The smoke from the blast lifting up pieces of the floorboard into the air. I was shocked for a moment, my whole body shaking, and then I heard it, the recoil of the shotgun. Heavy footsteps moved into the apartment and I froze.

"Get up, linda."

That voice was like acid running through my veins. I knew that voice well. It belonged to Carlos La Plaga Trejo. One of the most cynical criminal minds I'd ever come across and the man who had nearly ruined me as a child.

"Muevete!" He shouted, poking me in the ribs with the barrel of the gun.

I moved slowly, forcing myself to stand up. My legs nearly gave out on me while I stood in the middle of the floor, finding myself alone and helpless. His laughter grated on my nerves causing me to shudder involuntarily.

He stood before me, his scar prominent against his upper lip and cheek. His black hair was greasy, and it fell in long strands along his shoulders.

Raising the barrel of the gun he pinned the base of it under his armpit, pointing it at me. I turned my face and clenched my eyes shut. The metal piece slid across my breasts and I flinched as it flicked my nipple.

"You look all grown up, Cecilia. I bet those titties feel even better now, all round and swollen. Coño, you look good enough to bounce on my cock. I bet you can take this cock now, can't you?"

"You're disgusting," I grunted and coughed as he poked me hard in the ribs.

"Respeto!" He grabbed my t-shirt and dragged me up to him.

"Apparently your manners died along with your father."

I grimaced as he pressed his nose against my cheek and inhaled. "You smell... expensive."

"And you smell rancid," I hissed as he yanked my hair back. He pressed the barrel up against my chin.

"Where is he?"

"I don't know who you're talking about!"

"Puta mentirosa!" His grip tightened on my hair and the pain ricocheted down my neck, but I didn't give him the pleasure of showing it.

"When I find him, I'm going to serve him your pretty little heart on a silver platter."

"Make it gold, my man has expensive tastes."

My sarcasm was going to get me killed. At least this time it only earned me a smack across the side of my face that sent me reeling back. He grabbed my t-shirt and hauled me back.

"You are testing my limits, niña."

"And you're wasting my time," I spat out only to receive another smack, this one splitting my lip in two. The taste of copper coated my tongue and I laughed. I laughed because there was nothing else to do. Six years in hiding to return to this.

"You defend him even after what he did to you? After what he did to your father?"

"He was not my father." I glared at the man I hated more than life itself. Mario Cepeda was a man who only knew how to destroy, Carlos Trejo was just like him.

Wiping the blood off my lip, I glowered at him with so much hatred held in my heart. "He is going to murder you."

He lifted me up and gripped my chin, squeezing until I flinched from the pain. He smiled at me, that vicious scar looking rough and raw on his face. I closed my eyes for a second, not wanting to look at him.

"I will return your lover to you, cut up in tiny little pieces and feed him to my dogs. That is when I'll come back for you, niña. And when I do, I will have you on your knees with my cock so far up that beautiful ass of yours, begging me, like the good whore you are."

"Never!"

"Eh-eh," he squeezed my chin harder. "You will beg for me. You will scream for me. All while I remind you who La Plaga really is."

I could feel my blood pressure drop and my legs were going to give out on me. Suddenly, the roar of the motorcycles alerted us that the Death Row Shooters were on their way back. They'd told me not to leave, told me to stay put while they did a quick job, but I was never prepared for this.

"Hmmm, I think your boyfriend is coming home."

He grabbed me by my hair and forced me to kneel before him. He rubbed his crotch against my cheek and I clenched my eyes shut. If he wanted to rape me, he could easily do it.

Leaning down, he yanked my head back so his face was

only an inch from mine. "I'm going to own you, Cecilia Cepeda. I'm going to make you into my little slave and slide my cock so deep into you, you will forget he ever existed."

"Fuck you," I spat blood in his face and grimaced as he licked it off his lip.

"You taste sweet, baby. I can't wait to spit on that tight cunt and make it nice and wet. But first, I need to make sure your boyfriend pays for what he did."

"Not before he cuts your dick off for touching the President of the Death Row Shooter's Ol' Lady." I was oddly proud to hold that title, but it didn't faze La Plaga.

"That stupid bitch doesn't scare me! Get up!"

He dragged me up and I struggled against him as I realized he wanted to take me with him. I bit, I scratched, I screamed, and suddenly he swung at me sending me flying down to the floor. The roar of the bikes got closer. If I could just stall him. He lifted me up and just in spite, he bit down on my split lip. I cried out in agony while his hand gripped my core, squeezing.

"I am going to take what is owed to me."

I smirked. "You'll have to get through a clubhouse full of Death Row Shooters before you get to me."

He roared in anger and I saw the handle of the rifle come at me, it hit me on my temple and I crumbled to the floor. My vision blurred and all I could make out was the outline of his boots by my head. My eyes struggled to remain open as I heard the shouts heading my way. In my stupor I felt hands lifting me up and I slipped away into darkness.

19

RYAN

RYAN

OPENING THE CLUB DOOR, I froze. All I could see were his legs strewn across the floor. Opening the door wider, my body ran cold. Ash rushed past me and knelt by Mikey's side. His hands fluttered over his body.

"Is he dead?"

He stared back at me, anger blazing in his dark eyes. Mikey's limp form lay before him, a knife piercing his heart.

"Cecilia!" I roared running into the building only to find Zephyr strewn on the floor clutching his leg and moaning.

"Zeph!" I ran towards the new prospect, a young kid of twenty-one.

He gripped my jacket, his green eyes staring back at me in fear. "He took her. Walked right out with her. I tried to take him down. I tried."

I patted his shoulder and looking back I signaled for Shotgun to take him. I made my way to the third floor and stopped short. He'd blasted the door and as I stepped over the pieces, I saw drops of blood on the floor. Clenching my fists, I swore, I was going to kill the motherfucker. I sensed Ash behind me.

"What is it?"

"He wants a meeting with you," Ash shoved a piece of paper at me. Scrawled on the front was a message in poorly written handwriting.

Midnight at the docks.

I sighed and thought for a moment. My head was spinning with Cecilia in the forefront of everything. I needed to get her back, needed to know she was safe. I hated this feeling of having my hands tied. I was always in control.

Poe had left this morning with the damn shipment and Digger took Crow to help Walker Thorn, the President of the Devil's Syndicate, with a package delivery. It was a debt we needed to pay, and I wasn't about owing shit to anyone.

"I'm assuming he wants me to show up alone?"

"We'll be there with you no matter what."

"Call La Mancha. Set something up. I'm not letting this fucker go."

"Can't do that, Prez. We don't have the backup."

"We have no other options."

"We have the Hellbound Lovers."

I froze at the mention of their name. I knew that if I called them, they would come, at a price, and the price was too high for me at the moment.

"No Hellbound Lovers. I don't want them crawling all over this, it's our business and we'll handle it.

"But you're going to trust the Mexican Mafia to have your back before he kills you."

"What other choice do I have? Besides, La Mancha will be happy to hear that we're handing him over."

"I don't like this."

"You all need to stay back. No matter what happens he needs to believe he's winning. Let his guard down before we bring in La Sombra."

"What if the Hellbound Lovers start to question us?"

"Make up some shit!" I shouted at him, sick of his questions. Ash sighed, his eyes shooting to the ground.

"They're going to ask questions."

"I don't give a shit what you say just don't tell them what's going down!"

"I don't agree. I don't think it's a good idea to go in without backup. He may not come alone, the deceitful piece of shit."

I charged at him, gripping his jacket. "You either have my back or you don't! Either way, fucking handle it!"

Ash was my brother and I treated him as if he were blood, but he was on my last nerve today. "Just do as your told, Brother."

He nodded and went on his way, leaving me alone with my dark thoughts. Not only was Cecilia on my mind, my sweet girl who'd been battered in all this. But Poe was also on my mind. The fucker had agreed to go by himself to Hong Kong. Sure, Jameson was over there, but that fucker left his own brothers high and dry to go hide in an unknown country. How fucking trustworthy could he be?

I had one brother on a fucking boat headed to God knows where, another two taking a package carrying the fuck knows what to New York, and my VP who at the moment seemed to be against everything I had to fucking say. And my girl, who was caught up in this because of me. Things just couldn't get any worse.

REAPER

I arrived at the docks half past midnight. Ash, Shotgun and Jayce were already there. Ash had texted me only twenty minutes before I left to let me know they had eyes everywhere. The plan was simple. Stall. Make him think he had the upper hand and when his guard was down, that's when we'd make our move. Problem was, this fucker was off his hinges, and he could snap at any moment.

I carefully made my way towards the loading dock, searching the grounds as I went. The huge stadium lights we'd just put in, lit up part of the dock, but casted shadows in its surrounding areas. My phone vibrated and when I looked down, my body went on edge.

"He's here."

I walked cautiously behind the warehouses and towards the waterfront. Making my way around a crate I stopped short. There he was, standing in the center of the platform, my Cecilia in his hands. He snarled when he saw me, that evil glint in his eye letting me know what his plans were. I'd seen that look before right before he pulled the trigger.

"Welcome, Reaper," my name dripped sarcastically from his mouth. He fucking hated it, and the fact that it bothered him to that point, made me quite satisfied.

"I thought we'd buried you not too long ago?"

He chuckled. "You think I'd come back wearing that fucking patch. No soy tan pendejo."

"So, who was the kid?"

"Devil's Syndicate must still be looking for that kid. A prospect, I heard. Money talks so I paid the kid to ride on my bike wearing my jacket. You fuckers are brutal, the punk was only seventeen."

"Motherfucker."

"Walker Thorn buried his own and didn't even notice

it. I have to say I got lucky. Your man has good aim." His eyes looked up at the towers. "I'm surprised you came alone, Reaper. You've got balls."

He yanked at Cecilia and made his way down the ramp with her. Her eyes met mine, tears glistened in their depths while a rag covered her mouth. Her hands were tied up in front of her and blood ran down her temple. She was hurt, the fucker had hurt her. She struggled against him and he stopped, gritting his teeth. He yanked her head back and whispered into her ear, his eyes on me.

"Are you ready to watch me end the Reaper's life, mi niña? I guess in the end, I'll become the Reaper!" His sarcastic laugh made my blood boil and I remained quiet and stoic, staring at him beneath a dark glare.

I kept my gun at my back, itching to slide it out and pull the trigger. "Let her go. She has nothing to do with this. This is between you and I."

"And let her miss the show? Fireworks and all? I don't think so." He flung her to the floor, pointing at her, "You move, and I'll put a bullet through your pretty head."

She looked at him, horrified, but did as he asked. She continued to struggle with the ties but remained quiet. I looked over at her, my eyes reassuring. I was going to save her, even if I had to give my life for hers, but she was going to walk out of here alive.

"How do you want to end this, Reaper? I'll give you a choice, your head or your chest. Up to you."

I laughed. "You were always a vile piece of shit."

"I am giving you the choice you didn't give my brother."

"And I am promising you, I'll try my best to make a hole right next to him for you."

He snarled, reaching back for his gun and I charged at

him, tackling him to the ground just as he aimed it at me. The gun slid along the concrete a few feet away from us, and we struggled as I reached for mine. A swift punch to his right temple got him off me long enough to slide the gun out and cock it, but not long enough to keep him off. Grabbing a hold of my wrist, we fought for the gun. Tilting it forward we wrestled until he'd flipped us over, him on top, and I could see his eyes look down at me as the barrel of my own gun was now being pushed down against my chest and tilted at my chin.

Cecilia's shrill scream made me lunge into action. It was not going to end like this, I wasn't going to make it so easy for this asshole. I kneed him swiftly and he grunted falling forward, the gun slipped from my hands, but I managed to leap up into action. His fist met my cheek in one punch after the other. I staggered back for a minute but then regained my footing and swung back jabbing at air until I made contact with his cheek, then his nose.

His head flung back from the impact and he wriggled his nose and spit out blood. He smiled at me then, red crimson coating his teeth as he charged at me, his head butting my chest as his fists were relentless on my ribs. I grabbed him by his long wiry hair and jerking his head up, my hand came down aimed right at his nose. Blood spewed from it and he wailed, staggering back and covering his face. We both stood staring at one another, seething, worn out.

"You won't win, Reaper. You might as well give her up to me. I'm going to take her pretty pink pussy anyway. Right before I snap her neck. I bet she'll squeeze me real tight as I take her life away."

"Son of a bitch!" I growled as I lunged forward, swinging back and punching him on the side of the temple with the back of my fist. Then I came down on him again and again. He grabbed at me and in our struggle, I lost my footing. He managed to drag me to the ground, kicking and punching at me, just like he had so long ago. I struggled for breath as his foot met my rib, when he went to do it again, I grabbed it and twisted, bring him down to his knees. But he was incessant, and I knew that where we stood, Shotgun had no angle to get a decent shot. Ash and Jayce were probably on their way down even though I told them to stay put.

"After I kill you I'll have her as mi reina. Sitting on my cock, her new throne."

"Fuck you," I spat out as he dragged me up by my leather cut and punched me hard. I shook my head at the sting of the heavy blow. He pulled back his fist and I was so weak, my vision so blurry, I didn't expect the next punch and it sent me reeling back.

"Hijo de puta! Muerete!"

He wailed on me one punch after the other and when I was down and couldn't move, my face bloodied, my eye nearly shut from the swelling, that's when the sound of the engines finally cut through the silence. La Plaga staggered back as I got up on one knee. I started to laugh, a cruel, brutal, sarcastic laugh that I knew would grate on his nerves.

"Shut your mouth!"

I laughed harder as he shouted at me to stop. But it was a laugh that came out of me naturally. He'd let his guard down, and as La Mancha's bikes and people surrounded us, I saw the shadows move in the distance. Ash and Jayce moved in beside me, one of them helping me to my feet so I could stand.

La Mancha approached; it was the first time I'd actually seen him in person. He was covered in religious tattoos of the Virgin Mary and a cross that encompassed half his chest. The letters La Sombra were strewn against the side of his neck and in script, above his heart, the word Teresa encompassed his right pec. Two of his men surrounded La Plaga and I could hear the fear in his voice.

"Please, no. I'll do whatever you want, but please!"

They put him on his knees as La Mancha approached. I tensed when he put his hands on Cecilia. He whispered something in her ear and she nodded. Her eyes on me as he slowly brought her over to me. He stared at me long and hard, he was a lot younger than I thought he would be, maybe my age, maybe a few years older. "So, you are the infamous Reaper?"

I nodded. "And you are the infamous Miguel La Mancha Veritas."

"I believe this precious thing belongs to you." He pushed her forward and she fell into my arms, sobbing.

"Ryan," her voice brought me back, but I didn't want to look at her. If I did, everything I had planned on doing was going to shit.

I handed her over to Ash. "Take her to Ravenous."

"Ryan, please. Please, look at me."

I knew I shouldn't have, but I looked down into those pretty blues of hers. I was worn down, beat, and broken. I stroked her bruised lip as I spoke. "You won't be there long, Firefly. I'll bring you back as soon as I'm done putting this fucker in the ground."

"You don't have to do this," her small hand landed on my cheek and I flexed, keeping myself from falling into her warmth.

"Go, Cecilia."

"Ryan..."

"Go!"

Ash dragged her away, her cries echoing in the distance. I didn't want to let her go, but in order for me to go through with this, I needed a clear mind. Clear of her scent, her warmth, her touch.

La Mancha smirked. "I like you. This. This shows respect between us."

I nodded. "Likewise. You gave us the initial opportunity and we failed. We're now giving it back to you."

He turned and signaled to his boys who proceeded to drag out the chain on the pulley. La Plaga's screams reverberated along the waterfront as they slowly curled the chain around his neck.

La Mancha walked towards him and spat in his face. "This is for my daughter, cabrón." With a flick of his wrist the pulley was turned on, a slow agonizing wait hearing the chains pull and rattle as he was raised. The sound of him gargling as his life was slowly choked out of him was not as satisfying as I thought it would be. I watched as they hung him in the air, the chains most likely tightening as he got higher and higher. He twitched and tried to scream but, in the end, he would suffer a slow painful death.

A gun appeared before me. The familiar glimmer of my Glock was in La Mancha's hand. "If I am not wrong, I am not the only one seeking revenge."

I looked at him for a long moment and slowly, I took the gun away from him. Staring down at it I realized that this was the moment I'd been waiting for, for the last six years. Opening the chamber, I tipped it and let all the bullets drop to the concrete. The sound of the clatter echoed in the midst of his screams.

Cling. Cling. Cling. Cling.

I dragged the bullet from my pocket and stared at it for a long time. Carlos Trejo's name encarved on it with my blade. Sliding it into the chamber, I raised it, aiming it at his twitching body. His eyes bulging out as he stared down at me. He knew the end was near, the question was, would the Reaper take another soul?

So much unnecessary blood. You don't have to do this Ryan.

Her voice wafted through my thoughts and it was a battle within me to make the call. Go through with it or walk away. I waited a long drawn out moment and then I flipped the handle and shoved it at La Mancha. "You do what you think is necessary. I'm done with this piece of shit."

Digger turned to look at me. "Prez, are you sure this is what you want to do?"

My eyes never left the gangster's in front of me, a clear understanding running between us. "He deserves his revenge."

Taking the gun, La Mancha nodded in acceptance. "There's one bullet in the chamber. If you're going to use it make sure it counts."

Turning, I dragged my feet as I limped back towards my bike. I could still hear the chains rattling as La Plaga twitched and choked on them. And as we walked away from the scene, the sound of a bullet being fired ricocheted through the docks. The echo gave me pause.

Sweet redemption was what I had sought after for so long and somehow, I found it in that moment. The past was now finally gone, but now what? I'd sent Cecilia back to the hands of the Hellbound Lovers. She needed to stay there, for her own good. It was the only way I knew she'd be safe until all this was done.

But the questions plagued my soul. Would she return from Ravenous? Would she leave me when all this was over? I hung my head and let my brothers guide me out. It wasn't a matter of blood anymore. It was a matter of the heart that held me back from getting what I wanted. If she didn't return it was as if she'd hung me alongside La Plaga. This I was fucking sure of.

20

CECILIA

He was standing by the window, the last rays of sun gleaming against his bare torso, highlighting the colorful ink that adorned his chest and arms. Bandages circled his ribs hiding the rest of his tattoos from my sight. I knocked softly and he turned. He looked gorgeous in the light, his dark blue eyes focusing on me. His blonde hair had grown-the locks sweeping against the back of his neck. He was barefoot, wearing only his black slacks and I swallowed as my eyes travelled down the groove of his hips aligned with ink. My mouth went dry while my core soaked itself, begging me for him.

"Cecilia," my name rolled off his tongue wrapped up in longing. "What are you doing here?"

The right side of his face still held the bruises he'd withstood. Wolf had let me know that he'd been badly injured, but until there was word, he couldn't let me go. I left anyway. I was tired of not having a say in my own life. Finally looking into Ryan's eyes, I felt like running to him. Holding him. Instead, I stood in the doorframe. My decision had already been made since the moment I saw him again, and there was no turning back.

"I heard you were hurt. They didn't let me come see you."

"I didn't want you to see me like this."

I nodded. "Is he dead?"

"He had a debt to pay the Mexican Mafia. We just handed him over, they did the rest."

I nodded again, my eyes searching his for more. "So where do we go from here?"

"I don't know. Wherever you want to go, Firefly. You told me once that I wouldn't leave this place, but what has this place given me? Bloodshed, tears, living in fucking fear of my life for the last fifteen years. It taught me survival but at the cost of what? My own soul?"

I remained quiet because he was right. This place was haunted with cruel and brutal memories. Blood painted the walls, and tears stained the pillows. "Will you leave with me?"

His head hung heavy and he sighed-his shoulders slumped looking defeated. "They're my brothers, Cecilia. The only family I have left." His eyes met mine, turmoil and sadness blanketing his features.

"I'm also your family."

"Until I know they are safe, I cannot leave them"

I paused for a moment, my face must have scared him because he walked up to me and fell to his knees before me, wrapping his arms around my waist-his cheek pressed against my tummy. "Please stay with me, Cecilia. Don't go."

"Ryan." I hugged him to me and fell to my knees before him, my hands cradling his handsome face. The agony in his eyes reflected the one in my heart and I thought-why? Why continue to suffer when there was no need.

"I think we've both suffered enough, don't you?"

"I'm a broken man, but I'm yours. Make me whole again my sweet, Cecilia."

His rough hands cradled my face so gently and I fell into him. My lips brushed his softly, tenderly. His breath fluttered against them, and I breathed him in. "I'm yours," I whispered, and his breath caught, his arms tightening around me and dragging me up and into his arms.

He lay me on the bed and looked down at me, the look in his eyes was dark and hungry. "Mine," he growled right before his lips claimed mine. He instantly took over my senses, his hands stripping me of every inch of clothing that lay between us. I gasped as his body dragged along mine, arching my back, my nipples grazing his chest and tightening against him.

"Hmmm," he rumbled before taking a taut peak in his mouth and rolling it on his tongue. Gripping his hair, I gave myself to him.

He bit down on me, leaving bite marks on the swell of my breast. Hovering over me he smiled. "You're fucking beautiful. You mean the world to me, Cecilia."

"And you are my world, Ryan. You always have been."

I cried out as he filled me, stretching me tight. Lifting my hips in the air, I received him, my pussy swallowing every inch of him. Excitement coursed through my body and I whimpered as he slid out, leaving only the tip buried inside. He rocked his hips lightly, teasing me as he leaned back, his thumb finding my clit. He groaned as he stroked and circled my sensitive button.

"Ryan," I breathed as my hips rotated along his cock. Sliding down to capture more of him.

"Yes, baby. I love watching you fuck me. Fuck your cock, sweet girl. Cum all over it."

He rocked only the first few inches into me, his deep circular motions building pressure against me. I cried out, clutching the sheets. He groaned and sank into me, my body tensing as I came undone for him. My pussy walls rippled along his thickness and he cried out as I squeezed him.

"Fuck!"

His thrusts were hard and rough, sweat dripped from his forehead onto my breasts and he swept his tongue along my nipple groaning.

"God, you're so sexy," I purred as he continued his relentless thrusts. Shifting me to the side he entered me from behind. Our body sliding against each other, holding tight as we drove one another towards that ledge.

"Let yourself go, Cecilia."

"Yes! God, yes!" I came once again crying out as his dick swelled inside of me, releasing his hot cum. His fingers played at my clit, teasing me and making my body spasm around him. His arms held onto me tightly while he continued to rock his hips slowly. We both moaned in satisfaction.

"Fuck, I love doing that to you."

I giggled and sighed. "Well, you do that really well."

"Are you sure you're staying," he cuddled me. His chin nudging my shoulder.

"Nnngh, well there's nowhere I have to be at the moment."

He bit down gently on my shoulder and I squealed and laughed while he hugged me. "You won't leave me if shit goes down?"

"As long as you don't leave me."

Kissing my cheek and my neck. His beard tickling my sensitive skin. "Never."

"I love the feel of you," I whispered.

Slowly he slid out of me and we both gave out a groan as he left me. I turned to him, my leg curling around his hip, his fingertips sliding down my back.

"Is it over?"

He tensed beneath me and I leaned up and stared at him. "I don't know, Cecilia. All I know is that I want you by my side."

"If I stay with you, you have to let me be."

"What does that even mean?"

"It means I want to work at the hospital. I want to have a normal life. I want to be your Ol' Lady, and have a ring on my finger."

He smiled as I spoke and stroked my cheek. "And a baby in your belly. My baby."

My eyes went wide, not really expecting that from him. "You want a baby?"

He nodded. "I want our baby. I want a family with you, Firefly."

My heart fluttered, and I leaned down pressing a sweet laden kiss to his lips. "I love you."

"You'll never be loved by anyone as much as I love you, Firefly. Promise me you'll always remember that?"

His words were said in earnest, his eyes turbulent, swirls of a stormy sea that yearned for calm. For some reason I felt like he was keeping something from me, or maybe it was just my paranoia. All I knew was that I was staying by his side no matter what. I tried to escape and that was of no use and the last few days only proved how much I'd missed him. I wasn't leaving him-for the life of me I couldn't. Life just wasn't fair that way and I had to make the decision. Die with him or without him, but either way, I would always be at my lover's mercy. That's just how it had to be.

"I promise."

He kissed me then and I got lost in his kiss. I could only hope it would always be like this with him. He was my safe haven. I had given my soul to the Reaper and he was the only one who I trusted to keep it safe.

FIRST EPILOGUE

CECILIA

Two Weeks Later...

I whimpered on his cock as I slid my pussy down onto it. We were in the front seat of the Cage and he'd teased me mercilessly until I was climbing over him and sliding my slickened pussy down his dick. He hissed as I rode him, my tits out on display, the sight of them bouncing made him growl. His deep rumble alerting me to how much he liked this. I leaned back on the steering wheel as he humped up at me.

"Your fucking pussy's gonna be the death of me, baby. What the fuck are you doing to me?"

I giggled as I clenched my walls on him and received a hearty groan in return. "Fuck me, Ryan. I need your cock in me today."

"You need my cock in you every day," he grunted as he gave me what I wanted.

"Take it, baby girl. Take that fucking cock," his jaw clenched as I whimpered his name. He loved my whimpers, said they made his cock pulse, so I made sure I whimpered in his ear, losing control as his dick slid in deeper and harder.

"I swear to God I'm going to spray this tight little pussy with so much fucking seed today." I groaned and bounced harder on his thick shaft.

"This pussy likes to feel dirty, she likes to be my tight little whore."

"Ohhh, yes, Ryan!" I groped my breasts, squeezing and pinching the tips as my body rocked on his. He flipped the door open and I yelped, wrapping my legs around his waist and holding onto him as he slid out. He propped me down, twirled me around and bent me over the hood, the bright sun beaming down on us and heating up my skin. He slapped my ass for good measure before sliding his dick deep inside.

My thighs trembled as he took control, because my man always took control. I only got a little bit until I drove him wild, and fuck did I love driving his cock hard and wild with need.

"Fuck," his heavy balls slapped against my ass and I moaned, leaning forward. He liked to have me like this, his hand wrapped around my hair, the other spanking me as he called me his dirty little girl. His dirty little Firefly. I loved it all, everything he gave me. And he made sure to always give me everything.

We'd talked about having children, and after that he'd claimed me as his Ol' Lady officially, even though he'd already done it long ago. But there were things left pending before we could marry. He wanted everything to be perfect, and even though he couldn't guarantee me a life without blood being spilled, he said he could at least offer me peace. I took whatever he gave me knowing that in the end, I was his.

"Fuck me," I yelped as he tugged on my hair, biting my shoulder.

His cock drove me wild, stretching me just right as he drove into me. He was rough and gentle, sweet and dirty, and he was a generous lover, making sure he'd make me cum on his cock before he even thought of relieving himself. Who would have thought the Reaper, thought a brutal criminal by so many, was also the sweet man with a heart of gold? My sweet man. My savior.

He took me how he wanted, but he also went through with his promises. A week after La Plaga's death I was allowed my freedom with one condition, he was aware of my schedule. After I got a job in a nearby clinic, he went with me to make his presence known. The other nurses loved it. His charisma won them over and with giggles and blushes they promised to let him know if I was a bad girl. Shaking my head, I had kicked him out.

He made sure I was taken care of, that I was safe, and I was okay with that. There was only one problem and it was that my man was keeping secrets from me. That's why we were out here. That was the point of this ride into the middle of nowhere. If he wasn't going to tell me, I was going to find it out my way.

Taking my chance, I turned on him. He slid out of me as I pushed him away, and I had to forget the instinct I felt to get off. Instead I focused on him. Dragging my nails down his chest I fell to my knees before him.

"What are you doing?"

I stared up at him as I stroked him, and he hung his head back and groaned. "I want to taste you, baby."

His hooded gaze was ridden in lust as I played with it. "Are you going to put it in your mouth?"

I shrugged and tugged him a little faster. "Are you going

to tell me the truth?" I licked at it lightly and he slammed his fists on the top of the truck, leaning towards me.

"Fuck, baby. What truth?" He hissed as I dragged my tongue along the base.

"Why are you so tense?"

He clenched his jaw, his eyes darkening. "Is this why you brought me out here?"

I wrapped my lips around him and moaned. "Mmhmm."

"Fuuuuck! There is no truth."

"Liar," I suckled on him lightly and he humped at me. I pulled back and grinned.

"Tell me the truth baby and I'll let you cream on my tongue."

"Fuck, Firefly."

I wrapped my lips around him and sucked. "Tell me."

"It's Poe. I haven't heard from Poe in almost a month."

"Uh-huh," I licked him like a nice wet lollipop and plopped him in and out of my mouth.

"You are a fucking tease."

"And?"

"And, nothing. There's nothing else to tell." He grabbed my hair and tried to push me onto his cock, but I squeezed his balls and he instantly stopped.

"I know you're keeping something from me. You've been on edge ever since that night."

He looked down at me and clenched his eyes shut. "We made a deal with the wrong people. I'm on edge about Poe."

"What wrong people?" I licked his tip and he hissed.

"I swear to God, Cecilia."

"I'm the one with your cock in my mouth, baby. Be nice." I licked him again and I swear he grew bigger in my hands.

"It'll be okay. I promise. Shit, Cecilia!"

I slipped him into my mouth, sliding him down to my throat until my muscles closed down on him. Sliding him back out, I jerked him off and his hips began to move against my hand.

"Are we in danger?"

"You will be, ugh!" He groaned I slid him back in and choked on him.

"Am I, now?" I purred licking his cock.

"Fuck!" I squealed as he lifted me up and slid me onto the front seat. Spreading my legs his hand came down on me, my pussy lips loving the attention.

"More," I moaned, and he growled.

"You're so fucking dirty!"

"Mmmm, yes," I moaned as he slid back in. His anger rocketing us up into sexual bliss. His thrusts were powerful, one leg on his shoulder, the other up on the dashboard as he drilled himself into me, my punishment at his fingertips. But I loved every second of it and screamed as the orgasm flung me back. He grunted along with me at his release, the muscles on his body rippling from the force of it.

Growling he leaned over me covering me in kisses and rubbing his beard on my neck and breasts. I cupped his face and forced him to look up at me.

"Just tell me. Are we safe?"

He cocked his head to the side and sighed. "You'll always be safe with me."

I smiled. "Good."

I shoved him off me and scooted up into the passenger seat. "Let's go. I'm hungry and Cookie's making my favorite."

He shook his head and chuckled. "You're somethin' else."

"But you love me anyway."

I gave him a side glance and he finally let out a laugh. It was a lighthearted moment, but I could tell in the depth of him something was worrying him and knowing Poe may be in danger made me worry alongside him. I only hoped our Poet would come home soon.

SECOND EPILOGUE

RYAN

One month later...

We hadn't heard from Poe in nearly a month. Not a phone call, a fucking post card, a signal that he was fucking alive. Jameson wasn't answering his messages either. Both had gone radio silent. The red metal shipping crate that had come in last night had my name strewn on it, with lettering that stated CONFIDENTIAL. I stared at the box and looked at Ash who was standing on the opposite end of it.

Digger frowned. "What do you think it is?"

I shook my head. "I don't know, but I don't know anyone in Hong Kong other than Poe."

Ash shook his head, his eyes met mine and I could sense the fear in them. I think we all did, afraid to look inside.

"You wanna open it, Prez?" Ash asked me, watching me carefully.

"Might as well."

I stepped up to the metal crate and opened the lock that was attached to the sidebar. I had a fucking bad feeling about this. The shipment that we were in charge of had gotten to its destination about three weeks ago. A million dollars had been deposited into our account and Digger had quickly invested it. Only problem was, we were missing one of our own.

I went to slide the sidebar over when Shotgun placed a hand on my shoulder. "Let me do it, Prez."

I paused a moment, dread coursing through my veins. He slid the sidebar to the far right, the metal clanking, and slowly he opened the crate. It was pitch black inside. We couldn't even see our own hand in front of our face. That same whisper came from within, followed by a rough cough.

"Who's there?" I signaled for a light and Ash slapped a flashlight onto my hand. Flashing it into the empty box it landed on a body that was slumped over in the corner. The cough emanated in the confines of the space and another whisper that we couldn't make out.

Pulling out my gun I leveled it out in front of me. Carefully, I entered the crate, Ash to my right, Shotgun at my left, their guns raised and ready to fire. The figure shifted and attempted to sit up, when he did I noticed the tattoo that outlined his right arm. He was full of skulls and the poetic words of Rimbaud were scribbled along his forearm.

A thousand dreams within me softly burn...

I'd seen those words before, thousands of times, and I rushed over to the body. "Ryan," he whispered thinly as he wheezed out a breath.

"Fuck! Call 9-1-1!"

Ash pointed the flashlight at his face, a face marred in bruises and coated in dried up blood. He smelled of urine and days of not showering. Looking around we noticed he'd at least had bottles of water, the only thing we could find.

"Who did this to you, Brother?"

He whispered in my ear and with horror in my heart I looked at Ash. The simple word he'd whispered signified so much more. And in that instant, I forgot who I wanted to become, and the Reaper came crawling back.

Run.

ACKNOWLEDGMENTS

The Death Row Shooters truly challenged me, and during the time that I wrote it I received so much support from you, my fans. So I'd like to take this moment and dedicate this book to my readers who are passionate about my broken, gritty, gorgeous alphas, and who have taken their precious time to get lost in my words. Thank you.

To my ride or die girl, my amazing PA, Kristin Youngblood. I seriously can't do half this craziness without your support and your friendship. Thank you for pushing me and for being that shoulder to lean on. You're my rock. I love you.

To my girls, Zillah Raven and Zulfa Cupido, you girls are my my strength. I love you ladies. Thank you for all the hard the work that you do for your authors. I truly am so grateful to have you in my life. My ARC Team as well, who is always on point and just enjoys what I write. Thank you.

Last but not least, to my author friends who are always there for me. From J. Lynn Lombard who helped me at the very last minute, to my bestie Nikki Landis who I go to with all my doubts and craziness, I'm so glad to have you in my life lovely. Chris Genovese who always supports me and is an amazing friend, and Jax Hart who drives me crazy, but you know I can't do this without you babe. You guys are amazing and I'm so grateful for each of you.

So, with that said, stay tuned for more to come on the Death Row Shooters- The Poet is next and he has a helluva story to tell you.

ABOUT THE AUTHOR

Thank you for reading!

If you enjoyed Reaper's story, don't hesitate and leave your reviews. I do love to hear what sinful thoughts my readers throw my way!

If you want to see where the Death Row Shooters stemmed from you can check out the Hellbound Lovers MC .
Grab the complete series on Amazon here...
Hellbound Lovers MC Series

To get the inside scoop, teasers, new release reviews and dirty details of my upcoming series sign up for the mailing list!

My Synful Newsletter

ALSO BY CRIMSON SYN

HELLBOUND LOVERS MC

WOLF (Hell-bound Lovers MC #1)

GRAYSON (Hellbound Lovers MC #2)

RIGGS (Hellbound Lovers MC #3)

CAIN (Hellbound Lovers MC #4)

SETH (Hellbound Lovers MC #5)

GUNNER (Hellbound Lovers MC #6)

DIESEL (Hellbound Lovers MC #7)

KNOX (Hellbound Lovers MC #8)

SINFUL HOLIDAY NOVELLAS

A Wicked Treat

Dreams by the Fire

Sinful Valentine Wishes

Christmas Angel

STANDALONE NOVELS

Coveted Desire

Devious Heart

RAVENHEAD CORPORATOION SERIES

Dirty Obsession

Beautiful Betrayal

Filthy Seduction

Made in the USA
Columbia, SC
02 June 2019